THE BIG
Football Feast
ROB CHILDS

including
THE BIG DAY • THE BIG KICK • THE BIG GOAL

YOUNG CORGI BOOKS

THE BIG FOOTBALL FEAST
A YOUNG CORGI BOOK : 0 552 54596 1

PRINTING HISTORY

This collection first published as an exclusive edition, 1997

5 7 9 10 8 6 4

Copyright © Rob Childs, 1997

including

THE BIG DAY
First published in Great Britain by Young Corgi Books, 1990
Copyright © 1990 by Rob Childs
Illustrations copyright © 1990 by Tim Marwood

THE BIG KICK
First published in Great Britain by Young Corgi Books, 1991
Copyright © 1991 by Rob Childs
Illustrations copyright © 1991 by Tim Marwood

THE BIG GOAL
First published in Great Britain by Young Corgi Books, 1993
Copyright © 1993 by Rob Childs
Illustrations copyright © 1993 by Tim Marwood

Young Corgi Books are published by Transworld Publishers,
61–63 Uxbridge Road, Ealing, London W5 5SA,
a division of The Random House Group Ltd,
in Australia by Random House Australia (Pty) Ltd,
20 Alfred Street, Milsons Point, Sydney, NSW 2061, Australia,
in New Zealand by Random House New Zealand Ltd,
18 Poland Road, Glenfield, Auckland 10, New Zealand
and in South Africa by Random House (Pty) Ltd,
Endulini, 5a Jubilee Road, Parktown 2193, South Africa.

Printed and bound in Great Britain by
Cox & Wyman Ltd, Reading, Berkshire.

THE BIG DAY

ROB CHILDS

Illustrated by Tim Marwood

YOUNG CORGI BOOKS

With thanks to Joy for all her vital help and support

1 *Make a Date*

'GOAL!' shouted Tim Lawrence in delight as his powerful shot bulged the back of the net.

Andrew hugged his captain with excitement. 'Magic! 3-1 to us. We're in the Final now for sure.'

'Not yet, there's still a few minutes left,' Tim said, trying to calm him down. 'Just you keep our defence tight. We don't want to let them score again.'

The captain of the Danebridge Primary School football team need not have worried. They finished their Cup semi-final well on top after recovering from the shock of being 1-0 down at half-time. But it had taken two fine goals from centre-forward John Duggan early in the second half to swing the match their way.

'Congratulations, lads,' their headmaster praised them as they huddled together on the pitch afterwards. 'A well-deserved victory in the end.'

'When's the Final, Mr Jones?' Andrew blurted out. 'I can't wait.'

'I had a feeling you might be the first one to ask that, Andrew Weston,' he smiled. 'You won't have

to wait too long. It's just three weeks away now, so make sure you're free to play, everybody.'

'You bet!' Andrew laughed and then led the noisy charge back to the changing hut on their village recreation ground.

His younger brother, Chris, however, hung back shyly. He wanted so much to join the team inside, but instead waited impatiently with his grandad for them all to spill out again.

Although he had played in an earlier round of the Cup competition when regular goalkeeper Simon Garner had been ill, Chris still didn't feel quite part of the team. They were all so much older than he was.

'You should go in there and share in the fun,' Grandad suggested.

'It's all right, Grandad,' he said with a slight shrug. 'Andrew will be out any minute now.'

He scuffed his toes against the wooden steps, and Grandad could sense the boy's mixed feelings. Chris would be pleased for his brother, of course, but knew that he himself was unlikely to be picked for the Final.

He tried to cheer his grandson up. 'Well, I reckon Simon was mostly to blame for their goal today, you know. He should have held on to that ball

like you would have done, not just
pushed it straight back out to their
attacker.'

'Maybe, Grandad, but he did well
really in the first place to stop the
shot,' Chris said generously. 'He was
just unlucky with the rebound, that's
all.'

Privately, though, Chris rather agreed with Grandad's comment. He fancied himself a better keeper than his rival but, for now, just had to put up with the fact that Simon Garner was first choice for the school. He knew his own turn would come next season when Simon and the rest had left.

Any further brooding was rudely interrupted, however, as the door was flung open by Andrew and Tim having a friendly wrestle to see who could get down the steps first.

'Did you hear old Jonesy at the end of the match?' Andrew jeered, enjoying a rare little triumph. 'As if any of

us would be doing something else and miss the Cup Final. What a stupid thing to say!'

'When is it?' Chris asked.

'Don't you even know that yet? You should have been in the hut with us. What a laugh! Hey, Tim, are you coming round our house to play for a bit?'

'Can't. Got to get home, we're going out this afternoon. See you.'

'Well, Andrew?' said Grandad, repeating the question. 'If you won't answer your brother, tell me. I'd like to know too. I don't want to miss the match either.'

'Oh, sorry, Grandad. It's later this month, on Saturday the twenty-eighth.'

Chris saw Grandad's face fall, even though Andrew was too full of himself to notice.

'Oh, dear!' Grandad sighed heavily. 'I think we may have hit a problem, boys.'

'What do you mean?' asked Chris.

'I'm afraid it's somebody else's big day that Saturday too.'

'So what?' Andrew demanded. 'What's that got to do with our Cup Final?'

'It's fixed for the same date as

Elizabeth's wedding. Your cousin Lizzie's getting married that day, remember!'

'Oh, no!' Chris gasped. 'You're right. Mum was going on again last night about what we were going to have to wear for it.'

Andrew began to look seriously worried. 'Hey, are you two having me on or something? Because if you are, I don't think much of the joke.'

They shook their heads.

In desperation, Andrew sought a possible way out. 'Well, we've still got time to play in the morning and get cleaned up in time for church, haven't we?'

Grandad didn't know how to break the bad news gently. 'It's a morning wedding, Andrew, eleven o'clock, and I've a nasty feeling that your mum will insist that you're both there. All the arrangements were made months ago.'

The brothers looked at each other in silent horror. They simply did not know what to say.

2 Keep It Secret

'I'm sorry, but you're not getting out of it. You are both going to the church and that's final!'

This marked the end of another vain attempt by Andrew and Chris to persuade their mother to let them miss the wedding. Her angry words as they left the house still haunted them as they booted a ball about aimlessly on the recreation ground.

Chris wasn't even in the mood to throw himself around in goal the way he normally loved to do when they came out to practise together. 'More like she means it's *not* the Final, by the sound of it!'

Andrew snorted in disgust at the cruel double meaning of the word.

'There's got to be some way we can change her mind,' he said firmly, choosing to ignore the fact that they had pestered for days without it doing any good. 'There's just got to be. How's the team going to be able to get by without me holding the defence together?'

Usually Chris would have jumped

at the chance to mock his older brother's boastfulness. But for once he let him get away with it as Andrew slammed the ball into the wall of the hut in a flash of temper, almost splintering the rotting wooden boards.

Now did not seem a very good time to start an argument.

'It's no use,' Chris said simply instead. 'Even Grandad has failed. Mum just repeats to him what she's told us.'

'Yeah, I know, I know,' Andrew cut in, and then began mocking their mother's reasons in a high, squeaky voice. 'The boys have known about

the wedding for ages; it's not my fault
their football match happens to be on
the same day; we can't let Lizzie
down, she'll be so disappointed if her
little cousins aren't in church. . .'

Chris shrugged. There seemed
nothing more they could do. Mum
knew very well how much the game
meant to them, but she was determined the wedding had to come first.
She had even written to the headmaster to apologize and explain why
they were not able to play.

'When are you going to hand that
letter to Mr Jones?' he asked.

'What! Are you kidding?' Andrew
yelled. 'I'm not going to – and

neither are you. I've already thrown it away.'

'But. . .'

'Listen, I'm warning you. If you let on to *anybody* I can't play, you'll get thumped. Understood?'

Chris got the message all right, but still wasn't clear why it should be kept a secret. His face showed it.

'Don't look at me like that. There's still time yet, anything might happen. I'm *not* going to give up hope. Maybe Lizzie and her boyfriend will fall out or something and call it all off!'

Chris shook his head. 'It just doesn't seem fair on the rest of the

team, that's all. You know, acting as if nothing's the matter and then having to drop out at the last minute.'

Andrew flared up and angrily hoofed the ball far away into the distance. 'Not fair on them! I'm the one who's being dragged along to some stupid wedding when all my mates are playing in a Cup Final and winning a medal. What's fair about that? Why did she have to go and pick that day to get married?'

Chris gave up and trotted off to fetch the ball to let Andrew cool down a bit. As he did so, Tim and Duggie came running towards them.

By the time he returned, the three of them were already chanting the chorus of *'We're going to win the Cup!'* with Andrew's voice the loudest of them all.

'We've heard it's Ashford we're up against in the Final,' Tim added, breathlessly, when they'd finished. 'Just right for revenge.'

'Perfect,' Andrew grinned. 'They were dead lucky to beat us in the league match before Christmas.'

'Wasn't it 3-0 to them?' Chris chipped in.

'So? You weren't even there, so belt up!' Andrew glared at him, still cross. 'Anyway, they won't get a kick this

time. We'll tear 'em apart and Duggie here will score a hat-trick!'

'Yeah, with Simon in goal, you at the back, Tim in midfield and me up front, Ashford won't stand a chance.'

The boys laughed and continued to joke about what they were going to do to their opponents, ignoring Chris completely. He wondered how Andrew could carry on like he was, knowing he almost certainly wasn't going to be allowed to play when it came to the crunch.

At that point, seeing Simon approaching too, Chris decided he'd had enough. He slipped away and left them to it, doubting whether any of them would even notice.

But over the next few days Chris wasn't the only one worrying about the risk of letting the team down. Andrew was affected too, far more deeply than his brother would ever have realized.

As he had not missed a match so far this season, nobody else was used to

playing in his key position at the
heart of the defence, and Andrew
began to feel very bad about not giving the headmaster enough time to
try and sort the problem out.

His guilty secret was proving
harder and harder to bear. He knew
he was in the wrong, but he just
couldn't face up to the fact of not
actually playing in the Final. He still
hoped against hope that everything,
somehow, would work out all right in
the end.

If it didn't, he could only guess at
the trouble he would be in.

Andrew tried to bottle up such
fears inside, but finally it all became

too much of a strain. His stomach was so churned up in knots that one morning in school assembly, in the middle of singing the first hymn, he suddenly felt very weak and strange.

Before he could stop himself, or make a move to leave the hall, he was spectacularly and noisily sick all over the next two rows of children standing in front of him!

And much to his teacher's great dismay, too, Andrew was then sick again back in the classroom later. Neither was John Duggan best pleased, since most of it went over his maths book.

For everybody's sake after that,

Andrew was sent home, only for him soon to notch up his own sickly hat-trick in the bedroom.

'Really, Andrew, couldn't you have dashed to the bathroom in time?' Mum scolded, beginning the unpleasant job of cleaning up the mess.

'Sorry, Mum, it just comes on me so quick. There's no warning, like.'

'Right, my lad. We'll have you to the doctor's tomorrow then to see what's the matter. I should think at least a couple of days off school will be needed to help make sure you're fit for Saturday.'

'No, no, I'm OK, really,' he began

to protest. 'Apart from being sick, that is, I mean. If I miss school, I might not even get picked for the team...'

Andrew tailed off, realizing what he'd said, and sank quietly back into his pillow. His mother looked at him sharply, noticing how his face seemed to have turned even paler.

'What's that got to do with it, Andrew? Mr Jones already knows that you can't play, doesn't he?'

'Well, yes, b . . . but. . .' he stumbled, trying to hide the truth.

'Good, so there's no point in worrying your head over that now, is there? What I'm talking about, of course, is getting you well again in time for Lizzie's wedding.'

Andrew gave a low groan. That was not exactly the kind of news to make him feel any better at the moment!

3 Team News

'Good to see you back at school, Andrew,' Mr Jones smiled. 'And just in time for the soccer practice too! I was beginning to fear we might have to rule you out for Saturday.'

Andrew forced a false grin. When Chris had suggested his sickness was a perfect excuse to get them out of their terrible fix, he had almost given in to temptation. But his desire to

play in the Final was so strong, he'd returned to school as soon as possible, still clinging to the desperate hope that Mum would back down in the end.

The other footballers were especially relieved to see Andrew charging around in the practice after school with all his usual energy and enthusiasm. He didn't dare tell them, however, that he'd been sick with nerves behind the changing hut before the start.

Chris found himself on good form, making some fine saves, but his heart wasn't really in it. He guessed he would land in hot water too when

Andrew did finally have to own up to their secret, although he felt sure there was no danger of him being chosen in place of Simon.

Even so, when Mr Jones gathered them together at the end to announce the team, Chris still couldn't help half-hoping to hear his own name, despite everything.

'To be fair,' the headmaster began, 'I've decided to keep an unchanged side from the semi-final. Likewise, the two subs are boys who also deserve to be included in the squad for helping us on our way to the Final. One of them is young Chris here. It'll do no harm at all to have a spare keeper around, just in case.'

Chris heard little else that was said. He felt too stunned, and he couldn't bring himself to look anybody in the eye for fear they would see his guilt. Instead of pleasure, a great cloud of doom settled over him, and when Andrew raced off with Tim afterwards, Chris wandered slowly across to where Grandad was waiting.

'You don't have to tell me,' Grandad said, nodding with understanding. 'I could tell what's happened by all the fuss you were getting and by the look on your face now.'

Grandad too had been hoping that somehow things might sort themselves out, but now, he reckoned, was the time to face facts. 'Don't you think Mr Jones ought to be told the truth at last?'

Chris looked up at him sharply in horror. 'I can't, Grandad, Andrew would kill me if he found out I'd blabbed.'

Grandad sighed. 'Well, suit yourself, but it's for your own good. It's different for Andrew, he'll be leaving soon and this is his last chance. You've still got a couple of years of playing in goal here to look forward to yet.'

The old man began to fill his pipe to allow Chris time to think the matter over before he continued. 'And Mr Jones may not forgive how you seemed to be prepared to let him and the school down . . . you see what I'm getting at?'

Chris did, only too well. The mere thought that he might never be allowed to play for the team again was so awful he almost burst into tears.

'It's up to you, Chris,' Grandad said gently. 'But if you decide to, don't put it off until tomorrow. It might be too late by then.'

Mr Jones was just about to get into

his car to leave when he realized that someone was standing behind him. He turned round to see it was Chris Weston – looking very upset.

'My, whatever's the matter with you? I thought after hearing the team you'd have been dancing with joy. Has somebody said something?'

Chris shook his head. 'No, that's just the trouble. Nobody's said anything and we should have done.'

Puzzled, the headmaster waited for Chris to explain what he meant.

'I'm sorry, Mr Jones, really I am. I didn't expect to be picked so I hadn't told you.'

'Told me what?'

Chris hesitated, before Grandad's warning made him continue his confession. 'It's just that I can't play on Saturday. My cousin's getting married and Mum says I have to go to church instead.'

'Oh, dear! I'm sorry to hear that, Chris. What a pity! But I'm glad you've told me now at least. Better late than never, I suppose. Hmm . . . let me see, perhaps we could still keep you as sub so you get your medal, even if you aren't actually there. . .'

He stopped suddenly as a doubt crossed his mind. 'It's a good job your mum hasn't banned Andrew from playing as well then, isn't it?'

He waited for Chris to answer and confirm that all was well regarding his brother, but the boy just hung his head in silence.

Nothing more needed to be said. The headmaster now began to see what might have been behind those recent bouts of sickness and he tried hard to control his anger in front of Chris.

As for Andrew, however, Mr Jones had plans which would make that particular young man feel really sick!

By the time everybody had gathered round at Grandad's cottage later that same evening to enjoy a family

get-together before Elizabeth's wedding, Chris had still not plucked up
the courage to warn Andrew about
what he'd gone and done.

The two boys were sitting quietly
at the back of the room, with Andrew
too busy worrying about how to
break his own news about the team to
Mum to bother talking to his brother.
Suddenly, however, he lurched forward off his stool and brought up the
remains of his tea down behind the
settee.

'Oh, Andrew, not again!' Mum
squealed. 'I thought you'd got over
all that.'

The bride-to-be immediately became

rather alarmed. 'Do you mean he's done that before this week, Aunty?'

'I'm afraid he has, many times,' she admitted.

'Well, I'm not sure I like the thought of him being horribly sick like that right in the middle of my wedding service. It'd ruin everything for me.'

As they fussed around, Lizzie made it quite clear she didn't want the risk of having a sickly little boy in church, and a white-faced Andrew could see that Mum was beginning to weaken.

He seized his chance. 'Does that mean I can play in the Final after all,

Mum, and help Danebridge win the Cup?'

She eyed him suspiciously, half-wondering whether he could in some way be making himself ill deliberately, but then sighed. 'Oh, I suppose so. You certainly can't stay at home by yourself all Saturday morning. Mind you, I fail to see how you can be fit to play football if you're not well enough to sit in church.'

Andrew was hardly able to hide his smirk when Mum said he'd better see if Mr Jones could still find a place for him in the team.

'Oh, he will, somehow, you can bet on that,' he said, slipping a wink across to Chris, who was too stunned by Andrew's cheek to say anything himself.

'What about Chris as well?' Grandad spoke up, sensing trouble ahead now that the headmaster already knew of Andrew's little game. 'Mr Jones might like to have him there too.'

But Mum quickly squashed that idea. 'Oh, no! Sorry. I'm having at least one of my sons in church with me. They're not both going to escape.'

'Tough luck, our kid,' giggled Andrew later, out of Mum's earshot. 'Funny how things work out sometimes, isn't it? I shouldn't worry, though, I don't suppose old Jonesy will mind too much when he hears you can't play. He can easily pick somebody else as sub.'

Neither of them knew it then, but Andrew was soon to be in for a nasty shock when he found out just who that somebody would be. . .

4 All Change

Mr Jones wasted no time in calling Andrew into his office the following day. 'I understand that you are, in fact, unable to play on Saturday.'

Andrew didn't have a chance to wonder how the headmaster knew or even start to deny it before another bombshell hit him.

'That being the case, I've already changed the team and chosen somebody else in your place.'

'No, no,' Andrew blurted out, tears springing to his eyes. 'It's OK, honest. Everything's fine now. Mum said last night I didn't have to go to the wedding. I knew she would in the end.'

'So you admit you knew you might not have been free to play?'

'Well . . . well . . . y . . . yes,' Andrew stammered, 'b . . . but. . .'

'But you decided not to tell me until it was almost too late to do anything about it. Or perhaps even leave us all in the lurch completely by just not turning up on the day itself?'

'No . . . no, it wasn't going to be like that . . . I mean. . .'

Andrew dried up, sensing it was useless to try and defend himself. After a long, heavy silence, he attempted an apology instead. 'I'm sorry, Mr Jones. It's just that I wanted to play so badly, I couldn't bear the thought that I might have to miss the match. And I can play now, really.'

'I'm sorry too, Andrew,' the headmaster replied, less sternly. 'But I have to set an example with you over this. I can't have boys putting themselves selfishly before the team like you've done, whether you meant to or not. The team and the school are more important than any single player,

whoever he might be. Remember that.'

Andrew nodded weakly.

'I'm afraid you've had to learn your lesson the hard way. However, you can count yourself very lucky that I'm still going to let you come with us – but only as a substitute. We'll have to see then if we can bring you on at some point in the game.'

It was a tremendous blow to Andrew's pride, not to mention a great shock to the rest of the team as well when they heard the news that their key central defender had been dropped. But after learning the reason why, they would only give

him back their support in return for his promise not to take it out on Chris, who by now had owned up to telling Mr Jones.

'Serves you right, really, you idiot,' Tim told Andrew, summing up their feelings. 'That's what *you* should have done in the first place!'

The Cup Final was due to kick off at half past ten in the nearby town of Selworth, half an hour before Elizabeth's wedding ceremony in Danebridge church. The two official substitutes got ready in their bedroom on the Saturday morning almost in silence, neither wanting to

watch the other dressing in such different gear to go their separate ways.

Andrew already had the team's red and white striped football kit on underneath his tracksuit, and was checking the laces and studs of his boots before leaving to travel to the match in the school minibus.

Chris meanwhile was trying, without success, not to think of all the excitement he would be missing, as he struggled into his new suit and wrestled with his unfamiliar tie.

At last they caught each other's eye. 'You're getting ready early,' Andrew began, for want of anything else to say.

Chris shrugged. 'Nothing else to do. Might as well get it over with, I suppose. And this tie will take ages!'

They exchanged a grin, their first for some time.

'No hard feelings, Andrew?'

'No hard feelings, Chris. You were right and I was wrong, and here I am

going to the match and you still have to go to a silly old wedding. If anything isn't fair, that isn't.'

'Oh, well, can't do anything about it now, I guess,' Chris sighed. 'Good luck. I hope you get on the pitch and help us win the Cup.'

'I will. How can they manage without me? The first sign of trouble and Jonesy will whip me straight on to sort everything out! He knows how much they need me really.'

They laughed and Andrew left with a joke. 'Be good in church, little brother, and don't go being sick! I'll make sure they save a medal for you as well, don't worry.'

'See you later,' Chris called after him as Andrew clattered down the stairs two at a time.

That was going to be sooner than either of them ever imagined. . .

5 *Send for the Sub*

Despite the spring sunshine, Chris stood waiting miserably outside Danebridge church, his thoughts clearly elsewhere.

'Cheer up!' Grandad said. 'It's not the end of the world. There will be plenty more Finals to come for you in the future, if I'm not very much mistaken.'

Chris managed a weak smile. 'I

hope so, Grandad. I just can't help wondering how they're getting on, that's all.'

'Aye, lad, only natural. I must say it's crossed my mind more than once too since they kicked off.' He looked at his watch. 'That was about ten minutes ago now. They'll be OK, I'm sure. And if not, well, they've always got Andrew in reserve to call on.'

Five miles away, as Grandad spoke, Andrew was already ripping off his tracksuit and preparing to get into the action. Things, sadly, had been going wrong for Danebridge right from the start.

Within the first few minutes they had missed an open goal, had their own crossbar rattled and then, worst of all, goalkeeper Simon Garner had suffered a nasty bang on the head when he dived down among flying feet to grab the ball.

The game was held up while he received attention from Mr Jones,

who was more concerned to make
sure the boy was all right than
whether or not he would be able to
carry on.

Simon looked a bit groggy but insisted he was OK when he realized
there was a danger of being taken off.

'What do you think?' asked his
father.

'The best thing will be for you to
take him for a check-up at the
doctor's as soon as you can, just to be
on the safe side,' the headmaster
replied.

'Let him stay on for a while yet
and see how he goes, or he'll be so
disappointed.'

Against his better judgement Mr Jones agreed, but was soon regretting it. The next time the ball came his way, Simon fumbled it badly and then even let a simple back-pass slip through his hands.

'Right, that's enough,' he decided. 'I'm sorry, Mr Garner, but Simon will have to come off, for his own sake. He's obviously not quite with it. We'll just have to make do as best we can without him.'

He knew that was going to be easier said than done. But even before he could send Andrew on, Danebridge were a goal down. The headmaster had been so busy thinking about who could play in goal that he never even saw the shot go in.

'What on earth happened?' he asked Mr Lawrence, Tim's father.

'Poor old Simon dropped the ball at the centre-forward's feet, I'm afraid. Probably took his eye off it, fearing another clash. He's lost all his confidence now, I bet, not to mention his nerve.'

Mr Jones groaned. 'Right, Andrew, you're on. Go and do your stuff and make up for all the bother you've caused.'

The referee delayed the re-start while Danebridge made their changes. John Duggan reluctantly pulled on

Simon's green goalkeeper's jersey, while Andrew was able to slot straight back into his usual position. He was thrilled to be on so soon and relished the battle ahead with his team now so much up against it.

'C'mon, Duggie, do your best,' Andrew urged, knowing his friend was much better at scoring goals than trying to stop them. 'We can't let them get another.'

But they nearly did straightaway. Before the emergency goalkeeper could settle in, he was beaten by an awkward bouncing shot, only to be rescued by Tim getting back in time to kick the ball off the goal-line.

At that moment, Mr Lawrence decided that something had to be done if his son was going to have any chance of lifting the trophy at the end of the game.

'This is ridiculous,' he said. 'We have an excellent goalie as sub and he's not even here. I'm going to the church to see if I can get hold of him before it's too late. He'll be more use to us than to them, that's for sure!'

Before Mr Jones could stop him, he was gone, running off to his parked car nearby and working out how long it would take him to get there and back if he drove at top speed.

But as Mr Lawrence raced recklessly along the country roads, Duggie was fishing the ball out of the net after Ashford had taken merciless advantage of Danebridge's problems to score their second goal.

'What!' Mum exclaimed as Chris stood by her side, open-mouthed, after hearing Tim's father's amazing request. 'You're wanting to take my son away this very minute to play football?'

His sudden arrival had been equally dramatic, screeching to a halt outside the church gate where the bride's car had been expected to pull up at any moment.

'Please let him come, Mrs Weston. I know this must seem very rude of me, turning up like this out of the blue, and I apologize. But his team does desperately need him.'

Mr Lawrence was still trying to

persuade her to release Chris when Elizabeth duly appeared on the scene. As the bride walked up the path towards the church with her father, she was surprised to find a group of people blocking her way.

'What's going on?' she asked, as her bridesmaids fussed around her, all eager to make their long-awaited entrance into the crowded church.

It was left to Grandad to explain the situation and Lizzie gave a little chuckle. 'It seems I'm fated not to have my soccer-mad cousins watching me getting married,' she smiled. 'Come on, Aunty, this is supposed to be a happy day for everybody. I don't

want any long faces in church. Let him go and play, if it's so important.'

Chris's hopes soared but still Mum remained uncertain.

'But he's got all his best clothes on. . .' she began, sensing she was losing the argument.

'Don't worry, Mrs Weston,' Mr Lawrence reassured her. 'He'll be able to change when we get there.'

'Well . . . I suppose so, all right, as long as Lizzie doesn't mind. . .'

Chris gave a leap of delight. 'Thanks, Lizzie, that's great!' he cried. 'I promise I'll come next time you get married!'

They all laughed, much to Chris's embarrassment when he realized what he'd said, but Lizzie came to his rescue again. 'Don't worry, Chris, I don't intend there to be an action replay, and I can see from Grandad's

face where he would prefer to be too.'

Grandad began to make a feeble protest, but Lizzie brushed it aside. 'Go on, Grandad, off you go as well. I'm sure Chris would love to have you there in support. And now, if nobody has any objection, I'd very much like to go and join my future husband before he leaves! He must be wondering where I am.'

'We'll be back in time for the reception,' Grandad promised with a grin and a wave. 'Chris won't want to miss the food at least.'

It was only as they roared out of the village that Chris suddenly had a nasty thought. 'My boots! I haven't got any boots. Can we go back for them?'

'No time, I'm afraid,' replied Mr Lawrence. 'As it is, we'll be lucky to get you on even for the last fifteen minutes. Let's just hope and pray that's long enough to try and repair any more damage that might have been done since I left.'

6 Say Cheese!

Chris's sudden appearance on the touchline caused quite a stir.

Not expecting Mr Lawrence's trip to succeed, the headmaster had said nothing about it to the players at half-time.

He looked Chris up and down with a grin. 'My, you are looking smart! But now you're here, get that suit off, we need you in goal. It's amazing we're still only 2-0 down.'

The next time the ball went out of play, the Danebridge re-shuffle took place and Duggie bounded across in relief. 'Never thought I'd be so pleased to see you, little Westy! Now I can get back up in attack where I belong.'

Chris found himself quickly stripped down to his underpants before being re-dressed in his favourite green top with the black number 1 on its back. The spare shorts fitted him all right but, to his dismay, there were no boots his size.

'Sorry, Chris, you'll have to play in what you've got on,' said Mr Jones as he bundled him on to the pitch.

Chris hardly heard the cheers from the Danebridge supporters. He was too busy worrying what Mum would say if he messed up his best shoes to have any time for nerves about facing Ashford.

'Right, we can still beat this lot now we've got my kid brother in goal,' Andrew shouted, slapping Chris on the back in welcome.

In fact, it was mainly through Andrew's tremendous work in defence that Ashford had so far failed to increase their lead. Several times he had come in with vital tackles when another goal had looked likely.

The whole team now responded and

at last began to play the kind of football that everybody knew they were capable of. Quite swiftly the game took on a different pattern, with Danebridge getting on top and making Ashford fall back on defence for the first time in the match.

But then, as if to show how dangerous they could still be, Ashford suddenly put together a lightning raid. The right winger outpaced his chaser and whipped over a pinpoint cross beyond Andrew's reach, planting the ball perfectly in the centre-forward's stride for him to blast home.

Already with both their goals to his credit, he seemed certain to score his

hat-trick and clinch the Cup. But, to everybody's amazement, Danebridge's new young goalkeeper flung himself high to his right, arched his back and at the last possible moment somehow got his fingertips to the ball to knock it away from just underneath the crossbar.

'What an incredible save!' gasped Mr Jones. 'That looked a goal all the way.'

'It sure made my desperate dash back to Danebridge worthwhile,' Mr Lawrence said. 'Without Chris in goal that would have been curtains.'

Grandad beamed with pride, not regretting missing the wedding one little bit now. 'Well,' he said out loud to anyone who may have cared to listen. 'If that doesn't inspire them, nothing will.'

The team didn't let Chris down. Tim, his sleeves rolled up as usual in his business-like way, urged his players on to even greater efforts, refusing to let anyone give up.

They had badly missed Duggie's strength up front too for most of the match, but now one of his typical, brave challenges among a ruck of bodies helped Danebridge pull a goal back.

Winning the ball forcibly in a goal-mouth scramble, Duggie turned it smack into the path of his captain, lurking on the edge of the penalty area for just such a chance to shoot.

Tim made no mistake. He picked his spot carefully and drove the ball low and hard to the goalkeeper's left and into the far corner of the net.

Dodging all attempts to congratulate him, he immediately dashed forward into the goal to fetch the ball himself and run back with it to the centre-circle, making sure Ashford couldn't waste any precious time in kicking off again.

But Ashford were still not finished. In what was now a rare attack of their own, a snap shot from long range took a wicked deflection off another player to catch Chris going the wrong way, off balance. Once again, however, Danebridge were grateful for his quick reflexes, as he managed to twist round to grab the ball just before it crossed the line.

'Great stuff! Saved us again, little brother,' Andrew grinned, and then

glanced down as Chris kicked the ball clear. 'I wouldn't like to be in your shoes, though, when Mum sees them!'

Chris gulped when he saw the state they were in. 'Oh, well! It'll be worth it, if only we can win the Cup.'

But time now was very much against them, and the referee checked his watch carefully when Danebridge won yet another corner. Tim saw him and decided it was now or never.

He waved everybody upfield, knowing it was worth the risk of allowing Ashford to break away and score again. The game was already lost anyway, if Danebridge couldn't equalize.

Apart from Chris at the far end of the pitch, every single player was crammed into Ashford's penalty area as Tim himself took the corner and swung it, head-high, into the goalmouth.

Andrew's heading ability was normally only used for clearing the ball out of danger away from his own goal, but now it was seen to far more deadly effect. Circling round to try and confuse his marker, he suddenly burst clear of him as Tim struck the ball.

It could not have worked out better if they had practised it for months!

Andrew met the ball firmly with his

forehead and it sped like a guided missile into the goal, exploding into the netting before the helpless keeper could make any move to stop it.

Cheers and groans erupted from the crowd around the pitch as Andrew found himself buried and almost suffocated under a mob of red-striped shirts. It was his very first goal for the school team – and his last.

'Wow!' he gasped when given a chance to breathe. 'If that's what happens when you score, I don't think I'll dare do it again!'

There wasn't even time to re-start the game before the final whistle blew, to the great disappointment of the Ashford players who had seen victory snatched from their grasp at the last possible moment.

'When's the replay?' Andrew demanded. 'I can't wait to get at 'em again.'

'There isn't one,' Tim answered him.

'What! OK then, we'll stuff them in extra time instead. Even better! They're finished.'

'No extra time either. That's it, we're all finished now.'

Mr Jones soon confirmed what Tim had said. 'I think a draw's the fair result in the end after all our

problems early on. Nobody really deserved to lose such a marvellous game. The trophy's shared.'

Tim and the Ashford captain went up together to receive the Cup, and the applause continued as all the players were awarded their individual medals. Even Simon reported back in time with nothing worse than a headache.

The two captains then had to toss a coin to see which school would be first to keep the Cup in their trophy cabinet.

'Heads!' Tim called and watched tensely as the spinning coin hit the ground and began to roll. When it

finally flopped over, his leap of delight left nobody in any doubt about who'd been lucky.

In the middle of all the excitement, Grandad had a quiet word in the headmaster's ear.

Mr Jones nodded and then called for order. 'Right, boys, no time for celebrations here. We've thought of somewhere else even better. Come on, all of you, grab your gear or we'll be too late. Follow me!'

Puzzled, the footballers did as instructed and a convoy of parents' cars tailed behind the minibus back to Danebridge. But instead of stopping at the school, the headmaster drove on past until he reached the village church where photographs were still being taken outside.

'Everybody out!' he cried, and it was another toss-up as to who seemed the most surprised at the team's arrival, the smartly dressed wedding guests or the boys themselves in their dirty football kit.

'We've brought the Cup back for you to see,' said Grandad in an effort to explain things to an amused Lizzie. 'Because without Andrew's equalizer and Chris's brilliant goalkeeping, the team would have lost.'

'It's our way of saying thank you as well for letting your sons come and

play for the school on such a big day as this, Mrs Weston,' added Mr Jones, before pointing down to Chris's feet. 'And I'm very sorry about those. That was my fault, not his.'

She stared down at his wrecked shoes and for an awful moment Chris thought Mum was going to be very angry with him or, even worse, with the headmaster. But when she looked up, she was actually smiling. 'Never mind, he was growing out of them anyway, and I guess it *was* in a good cause. I'm just glad he didn't have to play in his new suit too!'

And so a very unusual photograph

was included in the family's wedding album. It showed the happy bride and groom surrounded by a group of excited footballers, cheerfully holding up their medals as they posed for all the clicking cameras. They were also the only school team pictures that ever featured a pair of newlyweds!

'Well done, both of you!' praised Lizzie, as Andrew and Chris stood next to her, tightly gripping the Cup. 'I'm very proud of you.'

She bent down and, to everyone's glee, asked, 'Aren't you going to give the bride a kiss then, cousins?'

They immediately went bright red with embarrassment in front of all their laughing friends. But, after each had pulled a bit of a face, they remembered how much they owed to her and leaned forward, one on either side, to kiss her on the cheeks.

Grandad chuckled and turned to Mr Jones. 'I think they'd much rather have kissed the Cup, don't you?'

THE END

THE BIG KICK

ROB CHILDS

Illustrated by Tim Marwood

YOUNG CORGI BOOKS

In memory of Shane

1 Captain Chris

'Me? Captain! Why me?'

'Because, Christopher, I happen to think you're the right lad for the job,' Mr Jones smiled.

Chris Weston wasn't at all sure about that. He had simply been looking forward to playing in goal for Danebridge Primary School in the new soccer season. The last thing he had expected was to be captain.

'But what about Luke Bradshaw and the others?' Chris asked, still

stunned. 'Most of them are a year older than me.'

'Age doesn't come into it,' the head-master said. 'I want a captain who can be trusted to set a proper example to his players on and off the field – somebody like you.'

Chris was thrilled but he feared

that his surprise selection might not go down too well at first, especially with Luke. And he was right.

'A goalie's no good as captain,' Luke claimed loudly to a group of the footballers later that same day. 'It should be the best player out on the pitch.'

'And who's that then?' Rakesh Patel put in cheekily.

'Me, of course!' Luke boasted. 'Who else? I'm gonna be our top scorer this season.'

'So? That doesn't prove anything,' Rakesh argued.

'Just watch it, Patel!' Luke warned, putting his fist under Rakesh's nose. 'Anybody here will tell you I'm the best. Right, you lot?'

It was more of a threat than a request for support. Luke glared

round at them fiercely and they did their duty by nodding.

'And I should have been captain. Right?' Again the nods. 'Right! That Weston's got it comin' to him now for this. You wait. Stupid old Jonesy's gone and made a big mistake pickin' *him*.'

As Chris lay slumped on the hard ground of the goalmouth, well beaten for the fifth time in the match, he might easily have been tempted to agree.

The season had already begun badly with two defeats in a row and now they were heading for their third. And to make matters worse, he realized that Luke Bradshaw had come to stand over him and gloat.

'Oh, yeah, brilliant captain you are,' Luke sneered. 'What yer goin' to do about this mess?'

Chris hauled himself heavily to his feet. Despite their age difference, he was nearly as tall as Luke and could look him straight in the face. 'It might help if you came back to do your share of the work in defence for a change,' he grumbled.

'I'm a striker,' Luke spat out. 'I'm here to score goals, not stop 'em.'

'So why don't you go off and score a few for us then?'

'Huh! I would do if you wallies ever got the ball over the halfway line to me.'

'That's not fair,' Chris said, fed up with Luke's constant taunting during the past fortnight. 'We're out-numbered every time they attack.'

Luke shrugged. 'That's your problem, Weston, not mine. You're the one who's supposed to be captain. Now if Jonesy had chose me in the first place . . .'

He left the rest unsaid as Mr Jones, the referee, trotted towards them. 'The game's not over yet,' he urged. 'Keep shouting your teammates on, Chris. Don't let them give up.'

Left alone as Luke went to kick off again, Chris grunted to himself. 'Team*mates*, he calls them! I won't have any mates left soon, if Bradshaw has his way.'

A voice close behind made him jump. 'Cheer up, little brother. Not

your fault. You had no chance with that shot.'

Chris swivelled round to see Andrew leaning on the goalpost, smirking. 'How long have you been there?'

'Just arrived. Grandad picked me up from school in the car,' Andrew said. 'Never knew he could drive so fast in that old banger of his. I guess he wanted to get back to watch you play as much as I did.'

Chris looked across to the touchline and spotted Grandad refilling his pipe. 'I wondered where he was. He's missed most of the game now, thanks to you being too lazy to catch the bus.'

'Hasn't missed much by the sound of it. 5–0, is it?'

'5–1 actually, if you must know. Rakesh scored.'

Andrew laughed. 'Danebridge are useless this year without all the old superstars like me. That guy was given a free shot at goal there. Now if I'd still been playing, he wouldn't have smelt it . . .'

'Belt up, will you!' Chris hissed. 'You're putting me off. I don't want to let any more in.'

He very nearly did straightaway. A centre from the left was only partly cleared and he was forced to make two good saves, one after the other. Chris booted the ball a long way upfield to relieve his frustrations, half-wishing he could do the same to Luke's head.

'Well stopped, our kid!' Andrew praised him, ignoring his younger brother's bad mood. 'You show 'em you mean to make a fight of it.'

Chris pulled a face. He knew the real fight he had on his hands was more how to cope with Luke Bradshaw's spoiling everything by his efforts to bully the team into turning against their own captain.

His goal was peppered with shots right up till the final whistle and nobody was more pleased to hear it blow than Chris. When he started to give their opponents three cheers, however, he wasn't surprised to get only a weak response and he slunk sadly over to the touchline.

'Oh, dear,' Grandad said, seeing the boy's face. 'Don't take it to heart, Chris. You tried your best.'

'Not good enough, though, was it? I mean, I can't go charging around all over the pitch sorting things out like other captains can.'

'Your team really would be in trouble if their goalie went berserk like that!' Grandad chuckled. 'Anyway, it's not necessary. You get on and do it your own way.'

'I wish I could, but . . .' Chris checked himself before blurting out anything to Grandad about Luke, '. . . but it's just not the same without Andrew and the rest we had last season.'

'You shouldn't say that. They're all in the past now. Give it time. You'll see. I'm sure things will work out fine in the end.'

'I hope you're right, Grandad, but how long's that going to take?'

As Chris trailed off to the wooden changing hut, Grandad stroked his

17

moustache thoughtfully and sighed. 'I don't know, kids these days. Problems, problems . . .'

He wandered across to his stone cottage which stood at the side of the village recreation ground and paused at the back gate for a few minutes to finish smoking his pipe. All of a sudden he winced and rubbed his hand gently over his chest, puzzled at the painful twinge he'd just felt.

'Ooh, spot of indigestion, I bet, all this rushing about,' he wheezed, tucking his still-warm pipe into his jacket pocket. 'Reckon it's time to go and put my feet up with a cup of tea.'

2 Help!

'Uugh!'

Chris's breath was knocked out of him in a loud grunt as he dived down at Rakesh's feet in the scramble around his goal. But he came up grinning and triumphant with the ball safely hugged to his chest.

'Great stuff, little brother,' Andrew called. 'To me now.'

Chris hurled the ball away and sucked in another deep breath. 'Phew! Just what I needed this, a good hard

workout on the recky with all the old gang.'

'All right for you maybe,' Rakesh muttered. 'I could have scored.'

Chris laughed. 'Can't let you do that or I'd never shut you up! Now clear off and stop goal-hanging.'

Rakesh Patel was one of the few members of the present primary school team allowed to join in the rough and tumble game the following Saturday afternoon. Mostly it was boys of Andrew's age, now at Selworth Comprehensive, glad to be free of homework at the weekend and wanting to run off some surplus energy.

Rakesh loped away but was soon back again, jinking down the wing with the ball before curling over a high cross. Tim Lawrence, last season's Danebridge captain, met it with a header just wide of Chris's lunging hands.

'Goal!' Tim cried in delight.

'Rubbish!' Andrew retorted. 'Post. Would have hit the post and gone wide.'

Since their posts were only a jumbled collection of coats, there was the usual lively argument as to whether or not the goal would count.

'C'mon, let's give it to them, Andrew,' Chris said after fetching the ball from the hedge. 'We're still winning.'

Andrew's face clouded for a moment then lightened again. 'Aw, all right, suppose so,' he grinned. 'We'll be generous – that's 5–2 to us.'

'4–2, you mean,' Tim corrected him quickly. 'That shot of yours was over the bar.'

'What bar? It was well in.'

'You must want your eyes tested,' Tim said, shoving him playfully.

Chris smiled to himself. 'Just like old times,' he thought as he hoofed the ball back into play to get everyone moving again.

He glanced across to where a black and white border collie was snuffling around at the bottom of Grandad's garden wall. 'Keep an eye on Shoot, please, Grandad,' Chris called out. 'We don't want him coming on the pitch.'

Grandad was supposed to be looking after their dog while they were playing, but he seemed more interested in watching the action than in checking what Shoot was up to. Pipe drooping from his mouth, Grandad made no effort to reply, and Chris was forced to turn his mind back on the game as Tim fed the ball cleverly through for John Duggan.

With people like the bruising Duggie on the loose, Chris had to have all his wits about him. Sprinting from his goal, he just won the race for the ball, pushing it to safety as they collided solidly and sprawled together on the grass.

The attacker's quick temper might once have easily flared up at being blocked like that by the young keeper, but Chris had gradually earned his respect. 'Next time, little Westy, I'll get you back, you'll see,' Duggie

grinned, helping Chris to his feet.

'Don't bet on it,' Chris said, rubbing his arm, but when the next time did come, neither was given a chance to prove their point.

With Chris out of position after making another save, Duggie was about to slot the ball into the unguarded goal when, to his fury, it was suddenly whipped off his toes by an excited pitch invader.

'Shoot!' cried Chris.

'I was just going to!' Duggie yelled angrily. 'He robbed me.'

'I didn't mean that,' Chris shouted, equally upset. 'Come here, Shoot. Leave it!'

But as the players began to chase around after him, Shoot kept on

bopping the ball along with his head, barking madly.

'Hey! Stupid hound, get out of it,' Duggie screamed. 'You stopped me scoring.'

'Can't you control your dog?' Tim demanded of Andrew. 'He's wrecking the game.'

'Shoot! Come, Shoot!' chorused both Andrew and Chris, but this only confused the animal even more as he scuttled from one to the other, jumping up at them.'

'Send him off!' Rakesh chuckled. 'Show him the red card.'

'Down, boy,' said Andrew crossly. 'What's got into you?'

'Where's Grandad?' Chris piped up, noticing his absence from the wall for the first time. 'I didn't see him go in.'

'Well he has, and he's let Shoot scarper,' Tim complained. 'Put him on the lead, will you, so we can get on with our soccer.'

The collie's yelping was growing ever more desperate as he began to dash backwards and forwards between the cottage and the pitch. Every time one of the boys bent to grab his collar, he would twist about to shoot away again.

It was Rakesh who was the first to realize. 'Hey, I think he's trying to tell you something, Chris. The way he's behaving, perhaps he wants you to follow him.'

Chris's anger towards his dis-obedient dog vanished immediately and he felt his stomach churn over. A terrible thought suddenly hit him like

a cold sponge. 'Grandad! Where *is* he?'

When Chris began to run towards the cottage, wildly waving Andrew to join him, the game was abandoned and the other players either stood around or wandered after them out of curiosity.

Chris hurtled through the gate and his legs almost buckled beneath him at what he saw. Grandad had collapsed and was lying flat out on the ground behind the wall, his hands over his chest and his face screwed up in pain.

'Grandad! What's the matter?' he cried, tears welling up as Shoot crouched by Grandad's head to lick his ear. 'Can you speak?'

To Chris's utter relief, Grandad slowly opened his eyes. 'Sorry, m'boy,'

he groaned. 'Came over a bit dizzy, like. Must have fainted.'

'Andrew!' Chris exclaimed as his brother knelt down beside him, white-faced, and started to loosen Grandad's tie. 'I'll see to that. You get inside quick and dial 999!'

3 Down in the Dumps

Light from a street lamp leaked through the brothers' bedroom curtains and settled on two sorrowful faces staring up at the shadowy ceiling.

'Grandad *will* get better, won't he?' Chris whispered from his bed.

'Course he will,' Andrew insisted, finding comfort himself in his own words. 'You heard the doctor. She said Grandad just needed to rest up a bit and take things easy for a while.'

They fell silent again, remembering how much Grandad had helped them in so many ways, especially in their sports. He'd given each of them a ball to kick almost from the moment they were able to walk.

'Been overdoing it in his garden recently, I bet,' Andrew murmured. 'When he gets back home from hospital, we'll be round there all the time to see he's OK and got everything he needs, do his shopping and so on.'

'Right,' Chris agreed. 'We can even finish off that digging for him as well. And let him have Shoot for company every day.'

'Yeah, good old Shoot – what a hero!' cheered Andrew, sitting up on his

pillow. 'Lassie couldn't have saved Grandad any better.'

The memory of that awful moment when he had found Grandad slumped behind the wall made Chris shudder. 'I thought at first he was . . . well, you know . . .'

'I know,' Andrew said softly. 'It seemed to take yonks for that ambulance to arrive. Was I glad when Mum came and took over . . .'

He stopped. 'Hey, how did Mum know what had happened?'

'Rakesh fetched her. He ran all the way here – said it was quicker than phoning!' Chris explained, then added, 'He's a good pal, Rakesh. I wish I had a few more like him at school.'

'Why do you say that?'

Slowly, Chris at last began to tell

Andrew of all his troubles over the captaincy. He felt he could talk about such things at a time like this without the risk of being laughed at.

Chris need not have worried. Andrew was in fact so shocked that he climbed out of bed and went to perch on the edge of his brother's. 'You mean your own teammates are getting at you?'

'No, it's just Luke basically, I suppose,' Chris said. 'But he's making some of the others gang up on me a bit, taking the mickey and that. They're scared of him.'

'Well I'm not!' exclaimed Andrew. 'Want me – and Duggie – to go and sort Bradshaw out for you?'

'No!' Chris almost shouted, jolting upright. 'That would only make matters worse. I'll fight my own battles, thanks.'

Andrew grunted. 'Humph! Mind you, I did warn you, remember, when old Jonesy chose you. I said some lads wouldn't like it.'

'OK, OK, but please don't go saying anything to Mum – and especially not Grandad,' Chris begged. 'I don't want him fretting over me right now. Anyway, it might be better for the team's sake, if I simply packed up being captain like Luke wants.'

'Don't do that!' Andrew gasped. 'If you give in to him, he'll think you're a softie and keep on at you even more. You can't let him get away with it.'

'No, I guess you're right, I'll think of something,' Chris sighed. 'But let's forget about *him* at the moment. Grandad's far more important. I just wish I could at least come up with the one thing which would be bound to make him feel better again.'

'What's that?'

'For him to see Danebridge start winning – and that might even help to solve my little problems too.'

They both knew that would be easier said than done . . .

And so it proved.

Danebridge lost again in midweek, 3–1 away, with Chris's mind more on Grandad, due home the next day, than it was on the game. He would normally have prevented two of the goals without any trouble, one of which he let slip straight through his legs.

As they waited in the school minibus for Mr Jones afterwards, Luke tried to show Chris up in front of the whole team.

'You're a rubbish captain, Weston, and you're a rubbish goalie too. We ain't got no chance with you around.'

'Leave him, Luke,' Rakesh cut in, signalling Chris to keep out of it. 'You know his grandad's ill.'

'So what! Who cares? C'mon, the rest of you, let's take a vote. Hands up all those who don't want Weston in the team.'

His own hand shot up into the air, daring anybody else not to do the same. Paul Walker, one of the defenders, rather shakily raised his

arm but somehow found his voice too. 'Wait a minute, Luke. I don't think Westy should be dropped, he's a good keeper really, it's just that . . .'

As Paul's courage failed him, Rakesh spoke up again before others were forced to join in the vote. 'I reckon we'd be much better off Luke, in fact, without *you* in the side. You're so slow, you wreck all our attacks.'

'Oh yeah! So who was it scored our goal today, eh?' Luke sneered.

'My baby sister could have scored that one,' Rakesh scoffed. 'But who was it who got subbed later as well?'

'Only came off 'cos I got crocked in that tackle.'

Rakesh laughed. 'Doubt it. If you ask me, Jonesy's sussed out at last that you're bone idle and selfish. You never pass the ball.'

Luke Bradshaw was furious. 'Who's asking you, Patel? Just wait till we get out of this old crate – I'm gonna do you.'

Chris could stand it no longer. 'Shut up, both of you!' he demanded, his cheeks flushed. 'No wonder we're doing so badly when we're getting at each other all the time. We'll never improve unless we start working together properly like we did last year.'

'Huh! Listen to him, he hardly ever played last year,' Luke cackled. 'We had a good team then with Simon Garner in goal.'

'Doesn't matter, Tim's lot have gone now,' Chris went on, refusing to be put

off, 'and it's up to us to show we don't
need them any more.'

'And how yer goin' to see we do that,
wonderboy?'

'Well, er . . .' In his desperation, a
wild idea suddenly flashed into Chris's
head like an S.O.S. flare. 'I guess we'll
just have to prove it by playing them
in a match and beating them.'

'Beat Tim's team! Don't make me
laugh. You and whose army?'

Chris had no time to reply, even if
he'd known what to say, as Mr Jones
chose that moment to pull open the
driver's door.

'Right, all in?' the headmaster
asked. 'Everybody happy?'

Judging by their faces, he wasn't at
all surprised when no-one answered.

4 *Or Else . . .*

'Shoot! Come here, boy.'

Hearing his name, the collie lifted his busy nose out of the undergrowth at the edge of the recky and looked up.

'Come, Shoot!' Chris ordered. He followed it with a whistle which only made the dog cock his head on one side, as if to question the real need for such an interruption.

When Shoot then went and buried his head once more into the long grass, Chris stamped his way across to him.

'Bad dog. Come when I call, will you?
I haven't got all day.'

It took the lead and a good yank to
get Shoot to leave whatever fascinat-
ing smells he'd found. But Chris soon
got tired of being pulled this way and
that by his frisky dog and let him dive
away once again on some other in-
visible trail. He looked around, bored,
hoping to pick out somebody he knew
before returning to Grandad's. He did
– Luke Bradshaw.

'Oh, no,' Chris groaned, but it was
too late to turn back. As Luke's grubby
red tracksuit emerged from the
shadows at the rear of the changing
hut, Chris saw that he was not alone.
Paul Walker came out behind him.

'What yer doin' snoopin' round here,
Weston?' Luke challenged him.

'Just walking the dog. Anyway, what are you two up to that's such a big secret?'

'None of your business, *captain*, so push off!' Luke snarled, glancing over to where Shoot's hindquarters were sticking up out of a clump of weeds some distance away. 'Seems that mongrel o' yours got some sense at least. Like us, he don't want you with him neither.'

Chris let the taunt pass, determined not to show Luke he was at all bothered by it. 'What's going on, Paul?' he called out instead.

He saw Paul check nervously back at the hut before answering. 'Nothing, Westy, we're just messing around.'

Before either of them could stop him, Chris brushed by and peered

behind the hut, spotting the gap in the wooden planking. 'Have you two done that?'

'No, we just found it like that,' Paul said quickly.

'The village team will be really mad if they think their hut's been vandalized,' Chris said, inspecting the damage. 'They might even stop us using it for our school matches.'

'So what?' sneered Luke. 'It's too draughty anyway.'

'It is now,' said Chris. 'That hole's big enough for somebody to squeeze through, I reckon.'

Paul grabbed a few pieces of wood that were propped up against the boards. 'Look, they're all rotten. They were coming loose so we were just

going to put 'em back in place again
properly.'

'Yeah, that's right. We're doin' 'em
a good turn, mendin' it, like,' Luke
sniggered. 'And when's Jonesy's little
pet gonna do us all a good turn by
tellin' him he don't want to be captain
no more?'

'Why should I do that?' Chris said, trying to stay cool.

'Cos you're rubbish, that's why. And cos if you don't a few of us will grab you one day and bend one of your fingers back till it breaks. You won't even be able to play in goal then.'

Luke shoved Chris as he spoke, pressing him up against the hut. But Chris had no chance to defend himself. Both boys were suddenly startled by a low, threatening growl.

'Watch out!' Paul cried. 'His dog's here.'

Luke stepped back in alarm but Chris reacted even faster. 'No, Shoot! It's OK. Quiet!'

The growl subsided to a rumble in Shoot's throat, but his eyes never left Luke while Chris slipped the lead's noose back over the dog's head. 'OK, finish, good boy,' he said soothingly.

'C'mon, Luke, let's go,' said Paul. 'I've fixed the hole.'

Luke tore his gaze away from Shoot. 'Right, you heard what I said, Weston. Think about it. Otherwise, some time when you're by yourself . . . no Andrew, no Rakesh, no Grandad around – and no dog to protect you . . .'

Luke turned and walked casually away, trying to make it seem as if he wasn't in any hurry. Chris was left fuming and bent down to stroke Shoot's head to calm them both down.

'Good boy, you sure came back at the right time for once then.'

Later that Sunday afternoon, when Andrew was making a cup of tea for

Grandad in the kitchen, Shoot suddenly jumped up from the floor and deafened him with his barking at the back door.

'Whatever's the matter with him?' Grandad called from the living room where he was talking with Chris.

'He must have heard something outside,' Andrew shouted.

'Let him out, will you, or shut him up,' Chris yelled over the din.

Andrew was fed up waiting for the kettle to boil anyway and followed the dog into the garden. Just in time to see a figure disappear over the wall on to the recky.

'Hey, you!' Andrew cried. 'Come back here!'

There was no chance of that. Shoot was already barking his head off between the bars of the gate, and by the time Andrew reached the wall the intruder had made his escape through another garden.

Chris had also scuttled out of the cottage to join them. 'Who was it? Did you see anything?'

'Just some kid in a red top. Come scrumping Grandad's apples, I bet,' Andrew laughed. 'He was lucky Shoot didn't jump over the wall and get hold of him.'

Chris grunted. 'I wish he had, if it was a red trackie you saw.'

'I'm seeing red too,' came an angry voice behind them. Neither had heard Grandad hobble down the lawn on his new walking stick, and they twirled round to stare at where he was now pointing it.

Graffiti had been sprayed right across the side of Grandad's garden shed in large, careless capital letters, the can of red paint lying abandoned on the ground in the panicky exit.

'The spelling's not much good,' said Andrew. 'Even mine's better than that.'

'It's not funny, Andrew,' Chris grimaced. 'I know somebody else who can't spell.'

'Why on earth should anybody want to write that on my shed?' demanded Grandad and read the warning out aloud. '*PACK UP OR ELSE* . . . What's that supposed to mean?'

Chris's face drained of colour. He didn't need three guesses to answer that one.

5 Challenge

Grandad's rocking chair creaked gently backwards and forwards as he sat listening to Chris explain about Luke and the hut.

'I wish you'd told me before what's been going on,' Grandad said. 'It's no good just bottling this kind of thing up inside.'

Out of habit, he reached into his pocket for his curved pipe and clamped it firmly in the corner of his mouth, much to Andrew's dismay.

'I thought the doctor told you to give up smoking, Grandad, after what happened. That's no good for you either.'

'Aye, you're quite right, m'boy. Pity! I rather enjoyed puffing on my old pipe when I had some thinking to do,' Grandad sighed. Then, with a twinkle in his eye, he added, 'But the doc said nowt about me not sucking it, did she?'

The brothers smiled and let Grandad suck away at his unlit pipe for a few minutes in peace until he seemed to reach a decision.

'Your headmaster was kind enough to come and visit me the other day, Chris,' he began, laying down the pipe. 'And he mentioned that some of the village team have had a bit of money stolen during recent matches.'

Chris turned even paler. 'From the changing hut?'

'Aye, you've guessed it,' Grandad replied. 'I shall have to report all this, I'm afraid. Fetch me the phone book, please.'

'Who are you going to ring?' asked Chris fearfully. 'The police?'

Grandad shook his head. 'Mr Jones – if he's at home. I may be wrong about the thefts, but I'm not going to have some little hooligan nip into my garden and start repainting my shed.'

He raised his hand to silence Chris's protests. 'I'm sorry, but it has to be done. We'll let the headmaster handle this now . . .'

Mr Jones was indeed swift to act.

'There's no place in any team of mine for a thief and a bully,' he told Luke Bradshaw in his office the next morning. 'You are banned from taking part in any further school sport here at Danebridge.'

The boy had refused to own up until Paul confessed to the headmaster how Luke had forced him to help make the hole at the back of the hut.

'He made me keep watch as well while he broke in,' Paul whimpered.

'He said he'd kill me if I blabbed.'

Paul was let off lightly after Chris had also spoken up for him, but it was too late for Luke to be forgiven.

'How right I was not to make you soccer captain this season!' Mr Jones sighed. 'I decided you didn't deserve the honour because of your bad behaviour in the past and now you've disgraced yourself completely.'

Luke attempted a shrug but somehow it didn't really come off. At lunchtime, after the news of his punishment had spread, he still tried to act tough, but the footballers sensed that the swagger had gone.

'You'll be lost without me,' he predicted spitefully.

'We were losing *with* you,' Rakesh mocked him. 'At least now we can start to enjoy our soccer again and show everybody how good a team we can really be, given a chance.'

Danebridge certainly didn't seem to miss Luke in their next game, avoiding defeat for the first time by drawing 1–1. Their better team spirit was obvious, with all the players willing to run their hearts out for one another. They were inspired, too, by finding their goalkeeper-captain back on top form, highlighted early on by one blinding save from point-blank range.

Chris felt, however, that he still had something to prove, to them and even to himself – that a goalie *could* lead a side successfully. He decided after the match that it was the right moment to reveal the secret plans he'd made

since that row with Luke in the mini-bus.

If ever they were to rid themselves of the haunting memories of last season, he reckoned, they'd first have to do a bit of ghost-busting!

'Well played!' he called out above the noise in the hut. 'Just listen a minute. Some people keep going on about how great Tim's team were and so it's about time we put that to the test . . .'

'Play them, you mean, like you said,' gasped Rakesh. 'I never thought you were being serious.'

'I'm deadly serious,' Chris confirmed. 'But not just play them – *beat* them! In fact, I've already gone and fixed up a challenge match.'

They were all stunned for several

seconds until Rakesh broke the silence with his usual huge cry of 'Wicked!'

Chris grinned as he saw his idea beginning to catch on with the others too. 'Tim thinks I'm crazy but he's letting Andrew skipper the Old Boys team. They're calling it *The War of the Westons*!'

'I like it!' whooped Rakesh. 'As long as your grandad's not the referee as well!'

Grandad was happy to leave that job to Mr Jones, but nothing could stop him taking up his old place on the touchline before the kick-off on Saturday morning.

It was bitterly cold, the strong autumn winds whipping through the trees on the recreation ground. But Grandad, determined to show that he was well on the way to a full recovery, intended to use his walking stick more for waving about than for leaning on. He was tightly wrapped up, however, in a heavy coat, scarf and cap, and from one of his gloved hands dangled a loose lead attached to a lively black and white collie dog.

Soon Shoot was barking out a loud welcome to the two teams as they spilled shivering from the changing hut, the red and white stripes of Danebridge mingling with the yellow and black kit Andrew had borrowed from Selworth school.

'Pity Bradshaw isn't playing today,' Andrew joked to Tim as they passed a practice ball between them. 'We

could all have warmed up by kicking *him* up in the air a few times!'

Tim smirked. 'Talking of fouls, just you remember which side you're on. Don't go giving a penalty away or something to help Chris out.'

'As if I would,' Andrew choked. 'He won't get any favours like that from me, don't worry.'

But when Mr Jones called the captains together, the brothers ran to the centre circle to shake hands and grinned at the strangeness of facing one another on opposing sides.

'C'mon, let's kick off quick,' hissed Andrew, shuddering. 'I'm freezing. It's OK for you with that padded goalie's jersey on.'

'I'll need it,' Chris laughed. 'I'll be

standing about most of the game having nothing to do!'

The school's green goalkeeper's top was something very special to Chris. He always felt a tingle of pride whenever he pulled it over his head and he wasn't prepared to give it up without a struggle.

He won the toss and chose to have the wind to their advantage in the second half when everyone would be tiring. 'Forget the cold,' he told his players. 'We've got to try and hold out somehow till half-time.'

As Chris took up his place in goal, he became aware of how many people had braved the bad weather to watch the match. But it was not only the crowd which made him realize how important this game was. He also

spotted somebody else skulking in the cover of the trees.

'So, Luke's here, is he?' he smiled to himself. 'I thought he might turn up, hoping to see us get thrashed. Right then, that settles it. We'll have to make sure he goes home disappointed.'

Chris knew what a setback a heavy defeat might be for him and his team, and how Luke would never let them hear the last of it. But he believed it was a risk worth taking. If they could actually pull off a victory, it might even shut Luke up for good!

Straight from the start, however, they found themselves pinned down in their own half by the strength of the wind and the Old Boys' determination to make the most of it while they could.

Time and again the ball whistled around the Danebridge goalmouth, but Andrew's men found Chris at his very best as he twisted and turned in all directions to keep them out. And when Tim did once manage to slide the ball underneath the goalie's diving body, there was Paul Walker ready on the line to hook the ball away to safety.

Chris slapped his defender on the back in relief. 'Magic, Paul! That makes up for everything.'

His new friend grinned. 'Thanks, skipper. I said I'd be right behind you from now on!'

6 Bouncing Back

Desperate for goals before half-time, the Old Boys in their yellow and black outfits buzzed around the Danebridge penalty area like swarms of angry bees. But the killing sting just would not come.

Duggie, of all people, was guilty of the worst miss. Finding the ball at his feet smack in front of goal, he crashed his shot up against the crossbar. He struck it so hard, the bar was still twanging several seconds after the ball had rebounded out of play.

Andrew spurred his team forward with shaking fists and frantic arm waving, unable to understand how they had so far failed to score. If possible, he intended to put that right himself.

The next time he received the ball, he was just outside the area and looked up to see Duggie and Tim both moving in for a centre. But he also saw Chris standing off his line, ready to cut out the expected cross. Instead, Andrew tried a lob over his brother's head.

'Goal!' he screamed, but then watched in horror as the wind caught hold of the ball and stopped it floating out of reach. Chris was able to leap, stretch back and claw the ball down to one side for a corner.

'No! Save of the season, you mean!' laughed Rakesh.

But Chris didn't want any fuss, despite all the applause from the spectators around the pitch. There was work to be done. 'C'mon, concentrate,' he bellowed. 'Mark their men.'

Too late. Duggie beat Paul to Tim's pinpoint corner, only to see his header flash straight into Chris's grateful arms.

'We're never going to score today,' Duggie groaned. 'He must have a ball magnet stuffed up that green jersey of his.'

The Old Boys kept up the pressure right until half-time but when Mr Jones blew the whistle, the score was still 0–0. They slumped together on the ground in disbelief while, nearby, their younger opponents were noisily jubilant. Not even the headmaster's warning that the match was far from over was enough to calm the Danebridge lads down.

'We've got the wind in our favour now,' Chris grinned. 'Let's go out and give *them* something to worry about at last.'

He should have known better. As Chris gave Grandad a thumbs-up sign at the start of the second half, he was forgetting that nobody could ever afford to relax against any side led by his older brother.

Andrew didn't know the meaning of giving up. He drove his players on again into the teeth of a wind which had increased almost to gale force. Winning the ball himself in midfield,

he knocked it to Tim who slipped a pass with swift, deadly accuracy into Duggie's stride.

The striker shot quickly on the run before Chris could smother the chance, although the goalkeeper still managed to get a hand to the ball. He deflected it slightly but, sadly for Danebridge, not quite enough.

The ball clipped the inside of one post, bounced along the line to glance against the other and then plopped gently over into the goal.

Duggie held up his arms in triumph. '1–0!' he yelled before being swamped by his celebrating teammates.

'We've got 'em! The floodgates will open now,' Andrew forecast confidently. 'This is gonna be a massacre!'

Chris feared the worst too, but even

the older lads found it very difficult
playing into such a powerful wind.
Any ball that was lofted into the air
simply blew back over their heads and
Danebridge were able gradually to
press them further and further back
on the defensive.

Simon Garner, Chris's old rival for
the number one jersey, became by far
the busier of the two goalkeepers.
Each time the ball was blown out of
play he had to run and fetch it, and
then belt it for all he was worth just
to get the goal kick beyond his own
penalty area.

From one of these, however, the ball
fell fatally to the feet of Rakesh, care-
lessly left unmarked. The winger
accepted the free gift with glee before

lashing it straight back past Simon's despairing dive.

'The equalizer!' screamed Rakesh. 'We've done it!'

Even Grandad was seen celebrating, waving his stick so much that it set Shoot off barking in alarm. 'Sorry, m'boy,' he chuckled, feeling foolish. 'Mustn't get over-excited. Doctor's orders, you know.'

Mr Jones checked his watch to see there were just five minutes left. Briefly, he wondered whether to finish the game early with honours even at 1–1, but let play go on. Although all the boys were weary, both teams were still battling away fiercely for the winner.

First it nearly went to the Old Boys. Duggie broke clear of the Danebridge defence but, thinking he was offside, hesitated and allowed Chris time to race out of goal and snatch the ball off his toes.

Then it was Chris's turn to launch his side on yet another attack. Finding himself on the edge of his area, he decided to use the great strength of the wind to send the ball way down-field for Rakesh to chase.

Taking a big breath, he leathered the ball with all the muscle power his leg could muster. His boot connected like the bang from a cannon and the cannonball itself was blasted high into the air.

'Wow!' Chris gasped aloud. 'I really got hold of that one.'

Carried by the gale, the ball covered an enormous distance before starting

to drop to earth deep into the Old Boys' territory, making Andrew back-pedal furiously to try and deal with it. Most of the defenders were glad to leave it to their skipper, but Simon panicked and charged madly out of his goal to lay claim to it as well.

Both players were also keeping an eye on Rakesh, who was rapidly closing in from the left, and in the swirling wind none of them could really judge just where the ball would come down.

'Watch the bounce!' Tim shrieked as it finally hit the ground not far in front of them, but his warning was in vain.

By the time Andrew and Simon realized the danger themselves, they had collided with one another and toppled over in an untidy, tangled heap. Untouched, the football leapt up high again like a runaway horse and

not even the nippy Rakesh could catch it.

There was no net on the goal to halt its progress either. After two more bounces Chris's monster kick sailed between the posts to the open-mouthed astonishment of all the players, not least Chris himself.

His own teammates were the first to recover from the shock and they ran back to mob their captain in delight. A dazed Andrew meanwhile could only appeal to Mr Jones. 'Is that allowed? Can a goalie score?'

'Certainly,' the headmaster confirmed. 'It is rare, but there's no rule against it.'

Andrew shook his head as if to clear it of a bad dream, but this was more terrible than his worst nightmare. Not

only were his team losing, it looked like his kid brother had gone and scored the winning goal!

And so it proved. When Mr Jones blew for full-time, however, he was pleased to see how well the older lads took their unexpected 2–1 defeat. To Andrew's great credit, he hid his deep disappointment behind an embarrassed grin and even beat Chris in calling for *Three Cheers*.

But after Chris had led the response, Andrew grabbed him. 'Just wait till I get you home,' he cried, and then laughed as Chris looked suddenly worried. 'Only joking. Well done, our kid. That big kick of yours was incredible!'

Chris beamed. 'It was a get-well-soon present for Grandad.'

They glanced across to the touchline to see Grandad dancing around with Shoot and letting the dog jump up all over him.

'It seems to have worked anyway,' Andrew giggled. 'So I guess I'll have to let you off this time.'

Mr Jones also had Grandad in mind. 'I expect you'll be glad to get back inside for a nice hot cup of tea, won't you?' he called out.

'Aye,' Grandad replied, 'but it's done my old heart a world of good to see the lads play such a grand match. A real tonic!'

The headmaster nodded. 'After a captain's performance like that from young Chris, the school team should go from strength to strength.'

'Just like me,' smiled Grandad.

'Reckon I won't be needing this any longer.'

He bent down and offered his walking stick to Shoot. 'Here, boy, take it,' he said, and the dog immediately grabbed it between his jaws, hardly seeming to believe his luck.

'He can carry the stick home for me,' Grandad chuckled. 'As Chris has found out, there comes a time when we've all got to stand on our own two feet!'

THE END

THE BIG GOAL

ROB CHILDS

Illustrated by Tim Marwood

YOUNG CORGI BOOKS

For all those who hope to become star players yourselves one day . . . may your dreams come true!

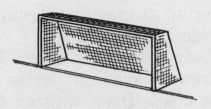

1　*Spot the Ball*

'I've won! I've won!'

Andrew Weston tore at his younger brother's bedclothes. 'C'mon, wake up! I've won!'

'Get off, you nutter. Leave me alone, it's cold,' Chris complained. He pulled the blankets back over his head, muffling his voice. 'What's all the screaming about? Won what?'

Andrew jumped on top of him. 'The *Spot the Ball* competition, dumb head. That one on the back of the *Corn Circles* packet . . .'

He was suddenly turfed off the bed on to the floor with a heavy thump as Chris lurched back up into view, hair sticking up at crazy angles and eyes now wide open.

'Are you sure? How do you know?'

Andrew waved a letter under Chris's nose. 'Been waiting for this for weeks. I knew I'd win. I worked it all out mathematically.'

'Mathematically!' Chris scoffed, remembering the picture on the cereal box of a goalmouth scramble. 'You mean you just scrawled in a few crosses and hoped for the best.'

'Rubbish! I drew loads of straight lines from players' eyes and saw where they met. Got it so spot on, bet I punctured the ball!'

'Hang on a minute!' cried Chris, sitting bolt upright. 'I put one of those

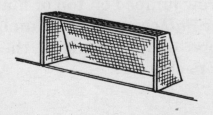

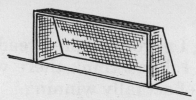

crosses on too. Could have been mine that won.'

Andrew shook his head. 'Nah! Yours was nowhere near. Anyway, it was me who made up the slogan they wanted as well.'

'You didn't tell me anything about that,' Chris muttered, knowing full well that his brother was bursting to boast of it now. 'Come on, then, what was it?'

'*Crunching Corn Circles every day helps me run rings round opponents*,' Andrew recited proudly. 'Brill, eh?'

Chris groaned. 'Sounds a bit *corny* to me.'

'Quit whinging, will you, or I won't pick you in my team.'

'What team?'

Andrew sneered. 'Here's you claiming the prize and you don't even know what it is.'

'Well, I never bothered reading the packet. I didn't think there was any chance of actually winning.'

'You see, that's the big difference between us, our kid. I always expect things to work out right and you just hope they won't go wrong.'

Chris pulled a face at him but the effort was wasted. Andrew was busy studying a notebook he'd pulled off the shelf above his bed. 'The prize, if you must know, is the chance to take part in a special soccer tournament. I've already got a wicked name for my team – The *Vikings*!'

Andrew grinned like an ape, hugely pleased with himself. 'Geddit? Vikings were Danes, right, and since we live in the village of *Dane*bridge...'

'OK, OK, I get it,' said Chris, trying to sound cool while his heart was racing. 'So who're going to be these so-called Vikings of yours?'

'Ah, well. There's Tim and Duggie of course – they've got to play. Then

8

there's your mate, Rakesh, he's good, and Simon as goalie . . .'

Chris dived out of bed. 'Simon! What about me? I always play in goal.'

He snatched at the notebook to see the names but Andrew kept it out of reach. 'That's the trouble, I'm afraid, little brother. It's only five-a-side, this tournament. I can't pick everybody, you know. . .'

9

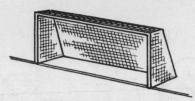

'He's just teasing you,' Grandad said when a worried Chris blurted out the news later that morning. 'You know what he's like.'

'But Andrew will want people his own age so he can win the trophy.'

'Nonsense, my boy. They're only a year or two older. It's ability that matters most, and you're a better keeper than his pal, Simon. Andrew knows that too, even if he may not admit it to your face.'

Chris brightened up. 'Do you really think so, Grandad?'

'You mark my words,' Grandad chuckled. 'What else did this precious letter of his say, anyway?'

'Weekend tournaments are being organized for different age-groups all over the country after Christmas, and ours is sponsored by United.

They'll have their scouts there, talent spotting.'

Grandad whistled softly. 'United! Andrew's favourite team. I can see now why he's got so excited. Still, that's no excuse for him to . . .'

Just at that moment Grandad was interrupted by a familiar loud knock on the back door of his cottage.

'Is Chris here, Grandad?' Andrew called. 'Me and the gang are just having a kickabout on the recky and we need someone to smash a few goals past. Simon's too good.'

He came into the living room, ignoring his brother's glare, and winked at Grandad in the rocking chair. 'Chris told you all about the Fives? Magic, eh?'

'Sounds marvellous. How many players will you need?'

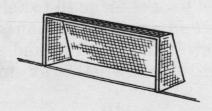

'Got to choose a squad of six, in case of injury or anything, but we're still one short.'

'Really? Got anybody in mind?'

Andrew pretended to think. 'Well, I reckon we might need another goalie, just to be on the safe side. But he'll have to come out and start practising pretty quick.'

'Oh, I don't think that will be too much of a problem,' Grandad said, glancing at Chris who was beginning to smile for the first time.

'Maybe not,' Andrew agreed, trying to keep a straight face. 'But there is something else that could prove a bit tricky.'

'What's that?' asked Grandad.

'Well, you see, we'll be staying overnight on New Year's Eve in a hostel near the city centre. The rules say we've got to have an adult to help look after us and act as team manager.'

Andrew paused and looked across the room. 'Doubt whether anyone will

be free then to do a vital job like that. Can you think of somebody suitable, Chris?'

Both boys began to giggle and Grandad's rocking chair suddenly stopped in mid-squeak.

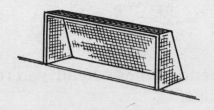

2   V for Vikings

The white football zipped over Chris's outstretched hand and smacked against the wall of the Danebridge village hall.

'Goal!' cried Tim Lawrence loudly.

Andrew turned the claim down. 'Hit the bar. Doesn't count.'

'How do you know it hit the bar?' Tim demanded, hands on hips like a teapot. 'We haven't got one.'

'Well, would have done, then,' Andrew insisted. 'The goals will only be about head height in the Fives, you know.'

15

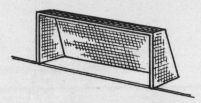

'Depends whose head you're talking about.'

'Belt up and let's get on with the game,' John Duggan cut in.

'Huh!' Tim grunted. 'You wouldn't be saying that, Duggie, if you'd just scored.'

Duggie smirked. *'Just because you're losing,'* he chanted tunelessly to rub it in even more. 'About 10-3, I reckon.'

'Nothing like it. I can see why you always come bottom in Maths.'

If Tim hadn't been the school soccer captain, Andrew guessed that Duggie's reply to that remark might have been made with his fists. Even so, he decided they could all do with a break and went to slump on a bench at the side.

It was the start of the Christmas holidays and Grandad had booked the hall to let the Vikings get used to playing indoors. A few friends helped make up a couple of teams, but Chris and Rakesh were the only boys still of primary school age. They went off together for a drink of water while the others began discussing the tournament.

'Can't wait for it to start,' Simon enthused. 'Just think of all those people we'll have watching us.'

'And United's scouts, remember,' Andrew put in, as if any of them needed reminding. 'We want to be on top form to catch their eye.'

'What a weekend!' breathed Tim. 'New Year's Eve as well and no parents or teachers around to stop

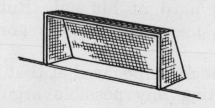

us having a bit of fun – apart from your grandad of course.'

'Oh, Grandad won't mind. He likes a good joke himself.'

'Look,' Duggie said firmly. 'I thought we were going there to try and win the trophy, not fool around.'

'Sure,' Andrew agreed, 'but I intend to have a few laughs, too, while we're away.'

'OK, just so long as we take the football seriously – field a full-strength side every match, no favouritism.'

'What are you getting at, Duggie? Are you saying my kid brother shouldn't be in the team or something?'

'No, course not. Just that Simon here is older.'

'So's Grandad,' Andrew said flatly, staring hard at his pal. 'But that doesn't mean to say *he's* going to play!'

Grandad reappeared at that point, preventing any possible argument.

'Oh, I see,' he smiled. 'I nip out to make a phone call and come back to find you all loafing about. Fine way to practise, that is.'

'Sorry, Grandad. Just talking tactics. What did he say?'

Grandad's face fell. 'Bad news, I'm afraid, boys. Mr Jones won't let me borrow the school minibus to drive you to the tournament.'

'What!' Andrew exclaimed. 'How are we going to get there now?'

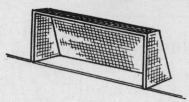

Even though they had left Dane-bridge primary school in the summer, they'd still hoped the headmaster would let them use the bus for something special like this.

Duggie could hardly believe it. 'After all the times we played our hearts out for his school in the past. The rotten old . . .'

Grandad cut him off. 'Relax! Before you say anything you might regret, Duggie, it's only my little jest. The good news is that Mr Jones has kindly offered to take us himself.'

The footballers cheered, but then a nasty thought suddenly crossed Andrew's mind. 'Er, he's not planning to stay overnight with us in the hostel as well, is he?'

Grandad chuckled. 'He's not that mad! He knows what you lot might try and get up to.'

20

The holidays seemed to pass very slowly for the Vikings. Not even Christmas itself and the first winter snowfall distracted them for long, and when they did finally set off on the Saturday morning, it was still snowing.

'Hope it doesn't get any worse,' Mr Jones said, peering up at the snow-laden sky as he drove carefully along the slushy country roads. 'Much more of this and I might have to cancel my return journey home today.'

Fortunately, by the time they reached the city two hours later, the weather had improved and he dropped them off right outside the hostel. 'Good luck, lads,' he said. 'Sorry I can't stop to watch you play, but I'll be back tomorrow to cheer you on then. Enjoy yourselves.'

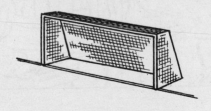

'We will, thanks,' Andrew called out, waving him off in relief and adding cheekily under his breath, 'especially now that you've gone.'

Grandad led the players through the front door and into the main lounge, where soccer strips of every colour and design were displayed on tables, ready to be collected by the teams based at the hostel.

Andrew held up a snazzy red shirt for the others to admire. 'This is ours,' he said proudly. 'It's my own idea

that I gave to the cereal company. I wanted it to be a surprise.'

'Wicked!' cried Rakesh. 'It's got a big white V on the front.'

'Right, that's V for Vikings.'

'V for victory, you mean,' Duggie stressed. 'Fantastic!'

The free kit wasn't the only treat in store. The sponsors had also reserved lanes for the footballers in the city's ten-pin bowling centre that night, to be followed in the morning by a guided tour of United's famous stadium.

For the moment, however, all the Vikings wanted to do was dash to their dormitory and try on their new gear. Reaching the second-floor room, they found it contained three bunk beds and it was Andrew, Tim and Duggie who won the scramble for the top berths.

'We've made it!' Tim cried, bouncing up and down to test the springs. 'Never let myself believe it was really true till we actually got here.'

Rakesh was soon posing in his red outfit in front of the wardrobe mirror. 'Which teams are in our group this afternoon?' he asked.

'Dunno, sorry,' said Andrew, kneeling up on the bunk and rummaging around in his sports bag. 'Grandad's got all the details.'

Chris, below him, popped his head up over the rail. 'Andrew?' he whispered. 'What's Grandad said to you about me and Simon? Who's first choice?'

Andrew grinned. 'Don't fret, our kid. You'll see plenty of action this weekend. I've not brought you along just as a mascot. Speaking of which – watch out!'

He suddenly whipped something from his bag and rammed it on to his head, uttering a loud blood-curdling shriek. Chris lost his grip and fell backwards while everybody else whirled round in alarm.

Andrew leapt down on to the floor
and went straight into a crazy, whooping war dance.

'Where on earth did you get that?'
Tim laughed, trying to keep out of
Andrew's way.

On the top of the captain's head,
slanting crookedly over his right eye,
was a plastic Viking horned helmet.

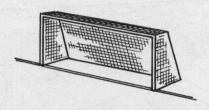

3 Group Games

'They're all girls!' Duggie exclaimed.

'What are *they* doing here?' demanded Andrew, equally disgusted, as they watched a team in bright yellow kit troop out on to the floor of the city's main sports centre.

Tim smiled. 'Why shouldn't they be? You must know that some girls are mad keen on playing football.'

'But a whole team of 'em?' Duggie said, shaking his head. 'Doesn't make sense. Who are they, anyway?'

Tim looked down at his copy of the programme. 'The New Stars, they call themselves.'

Andrew snorted. 'New Stars! That's a laugh. They're gonna get slaughtered. Pity they're not in our group.'

'We're on soon ourselves,' Simon pointed out. 'Or at least the rest of you are. Best get ready.'

Simon's worst fears had been confirmed when Chris was named in goal for the first game against a school side, Lynfield Road Juniors. Andrew saw he was still upset and wrapped an arm around his friend's shoulders.

'You'll play after that against those tough nuts, the Demons,' he explained. 'Think you might be a safer bet than Chris for that match.'

They'd just watched Dean's Demons wallop a local team, the City

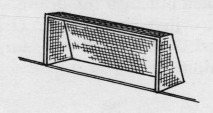

Boys, 5-1. Dean himself, a big powerful striker, scored three of the goals, and the losers had also finished the game with two players limping after a series of crunching tackles.

That wasn't the only reason that several of the Vikings seemed in a state of shock when they rejoined Grandad in the changing area.

'Whatever's the matter?' he asked.

'Those girls!' Andrew gasped out. 'They've gone 1-0 up against some rubbish lot called The Famous Five.'

'Great goal, though,' Rakesh admitted. 'Three neat passes, a clever one-two off the boards at the side, and she put the rebound in the back of the net quick as a flash.'

Andrew consoled himself by checking his appearance again in the long mirror before preparing to lead his team back out into the arena.

'Er. . . just a moment,' Grandad chuckled. 'Haven't you forgotten something?'

'What's that?' the Viking captain said, pretending innocence.

'You're not thinking of actually *playing* in that helmet, are you?'

As the Vikings kicked off their opening game, Grandad felt quite hopeful of their chances of success. They had two good goalkeepers to choose from, Andrew as the main defender and the battling Duggie up front, plus Rakesh and Tim linking things together in the middle.

By half-time, however, he was beginning to wonder. They'd been shown up by some fast, skilful, attacking play and it was only thanks to Chris being in fine form that the scoreline remained blank.

'No cause to panic,' Grandad told them in their brief get-together before changing ends. 'There's another seven minutes yet to get our own teamwork going.'

They needed every moment of it too. Especially when the Juniors took the lead straight after the re-start. To Andrew's horror, the ball was slipped through his legs, and Chris was well beaten this time by a firm drive from just outside the goalkeeper's semi-circular area.

This jolt seemed to wake the Vikings from their slumbers. At last they began to move the ball around with more freedom and gaps appeared in the Juniors' defence. Duggie was the first to take advantage of poor marking, sweeping the ball home from close range, but the winner came too late for anyone's comfort.

There were just a few seconds left as Tim weaved in and out of two challenges before putting Rakesh into the clear. The goalkeeper rushed out, but Rakesh kept his nerve and coolly slid the ball past him into the unguarded net.

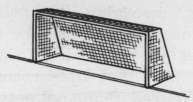

The scorer's reward was to be immediately crushed to the floor under a host of grateful teammates. They all knew how important it was to win this first game when only the top two teams in each group of four qualified for Sunday's semi-finals.

'Phew!' breathed Tim as they rested up while watching another match. 'We'll need to play better than that against those Demons next or we'll be in real trouble.'

He was right. Dean's Demons were soon swarming all over them and only Simon, protected by the goal area, escaped their bruising tackling. Not that he could relax for an instant. Shots were fired at him from every angle, almost making him wish Chris had played in this match too.

His rival was watching with Grandad from the side, both wincing at the frequent fouls. 'They're kicking everything that moves,' Chris complained. 'Why doesn't the ref make them cut out all the rough stuff?'

'I wish he would,' Grandad replied. 'It'd be better for their own sakes, too. Make them realize they don't need to play dirty to win. They've obviously got good skills when they want to use them.'

Andrew, on the other hand, was relishing being in the thick of the action, determined to show that the Vikings wouldn't be put off by such tactics. His own tight marking prevented his opposing captain from scoring this time, much to Dean's annoyance, but even his inspired efforts

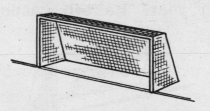

couldn't stop the Demons gaining a 2-0 victory by the end.

'I just hope we meet that lot again somehow,' Andrew said after the game. 'I'd love to have another crack at them.'

'What!' Simon exclaimed. 'You must be joking. I think they'll be giving me nightmares for weeks. Millions of green shirts all buzzing around my goal!'

'No time for nightmares,' Andrew decided, a gleam in his eye as an idea began to take shape. 'I think we'll have a little New Year's Eve party later.'

'Where? At the bowling centre?' asked Rakesh.

'No, later than that . . . much later. Next year.'

'Next year!' Rakesh gasped, and

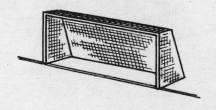

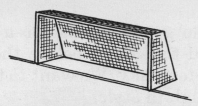

then realized what Andrew meant.

'Just after midnight,' his captain explained, 'while all the adults are watching telly downstairs, we'll celebrate the New Year ourselves in one of the other dorms.'

'Who's invited us?' demanded Duggie.

'Nobody,' Andrew winked. 'This is a surprise party. I just thought it'd be nice of us to go and wish the Demons a Happy New Year – with a Viking raid!'

Their final match against the City Boys turned out to be the decider for the runners-up place in the group. By then, Dean's Demons had already finished top with three straight wins and the Vikings knew they needed only a point to join them in the semis.

'It's no good playing for a draw,' Grandad told them before the kick-off. 'It's too risky. We want to try and go through in style.'

The Vikings did just that. Chris, back in goal, had little to do apart from pulling off one excellent reflex save late in the game when his team were already comfortably ahead. Tim had scored twice before half-time and,

after another goal from Duggie, he completed a personal hat-trick by steering in his third with the side of his left foot.

'4-0!' cried Andrew in triumph as the final whistle blew. 'Great stuff, team, I wonder who we'll be playing tomorrow?'

'The winners of the other group,' Grandad confirmed. 'I've just been over to look at the main scoreboard. Guess!'

Andrew's jaw dropped open. 'No, not the New Stars, surely?'

'Right first time. It was settled on goal difference.'

They all dashed across the arena to check that Grandad wasn't pulling their legs.

'I can hardly believe it,' gaped Andrew, staring at all the results.

'Time for you to make a New Year Resolution, I reckon, captain,' Tim smiled.

'What's that?' Andrew said, still shaking his head and only half-listening.

'You should promise never again to make fun of girl footballers!'

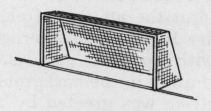

4   Strike!

All ten pins clattered over and Grandad bowed to the Vikings' shrieks of delight.

'Strike!' Andrew cried. 'What a bowler!'

'First time lucky,' Grandad said. 'And last. That's it, I'm retiring, I need a rest. You lot can get on with it.'

He chuckled to himself and sank back on to one of the couches around the computerized score panel. 'I'm just like a big kid,' he wheezed.

He'd never been in a modern bowling centre before. Bombarded by sounds from all sides, he was utterly amazed at the amount of electronic wizardry. Huge screens overhead pulsated with pop videos, game machines jangled away in the background and each strike was greeted by a great chorus of cheers.

Fortunately for Grandad's ears, that wasn't too often. The footballers had refused to use the long *bump 'n bowl* cushions and many of their efforts simply trundled straight off the lane into the gutters. It was a good job the computers *were* keeping the scores, he mused, as nobody else seemed able to add up properly.

Tim was the most accurate of the Vikings. Besides gaining the odd strike, he sometimes even managed to clear the remaining pins with his second bowl to record vital spares and keep his score mounting up.

'You're our main *striker* now, Tim,' joked Rakesh. 'Duggie will have to be sub tomorrow.'

'Watch it!' Duggie grinned. 'How many strikes have you got then?'

'Not many,' Rakesh laughed.

Duggie eyed the scores up on the screen. 'None, to be exact.'

'Oh, yes, I did. Look at the print-out from the last game. I got one there.'

'Wow!' Duggie sniggered. 'You'll really have Dean worried.'

Dean had proved the star of the show. He had a flowing, stylish bowling action and big white Xs kept flashing up above the Demons' lane to signal all his strikes.

'Why's a chicken come up on their screen now?' Chris asked after yet another strike met with howls and hoots from Dean's teammates.

'It's a turkey, dumb head,' said Andrew. 'Shows he's just got three strikes in a row.'

'OK, so it's a turkey. Anything to do with Christmas?'

'How should I know? I didn't invent this stupid game.'

Chris smiled. 'Don't get mad, just because you're no good at it.'

'At least I'm better than you,' Andrew scoffed. 'You're supposed to be trying to hit those pins, you know, not the people behind you.'

'I slipped,' Chris said in defence.

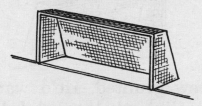

'I couldn't help letting go of it at the wrong time. Anyway, she wasn't badly hurt. She soon got up.'

The girl on the next lane hadn't been expecting an eight-pound bowling ball to come bouncing her way as she ran up to have her turn. She'd ended up in a big heap, lying half across the gutter, her own ball still stuck to the fingers of her outstretched hand.

As expected, when all the teams' scores were finally added up, the Demons were declared the winners and Dean swaggered up to receive a small silver trophy.

'Never mind, Andrew,' Grandad said as they watched them parade it around the centre. 'You can't win 'em all.'

43

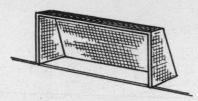

Andrew grunted. He'd wanted to wear his Viking helmet while bowling and had been upset right from the moment he'd realized he'd left it back at the hostel.

Suddenly he perked up. That trophy, he decided, would make the perfect target for their midnight raid.

'What a load of show-offs!' he muttered to himself. 'Can't wait to wipe those big silly grins off their ugly faces.'

As the church bells chimed in the New Year, the Vikings struck too.

Andrew threw open the door to the Demons' darkened dormitory and shouted his men on. 'Charge!'

His horned helmet led the pyjama charge into the room, pillows slung over their shoulders ready for the opening swipes. Sadly for the Vikings, however, the Demons had not been fast asleep. Instead, their intended victims were wide awake, tucking in to a midnight feast of sweets, drinks and chocolate.

The attackers made the most of their brief advantage of surprise. First came the volley of snowballs they'd scooped off the fire escape steps, aimed blindly at the beds, and they quickly followed these up with some good pillow blows to the head as the Demons struggled out of their sheets and sleeping bags.

As the defenders began to pummel back, Andrew picked out Dean on the far side and fought his way through the crush of bodies towards him. Dean had remained up on the top bunk, kneeling over the edge and bashing

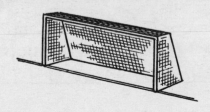

anybody who strayed within reach, friend or foe.

He repelled the Viking chief's first assault by knocking off his helmet and when Andrew unwisely paused to gather it up, Dean launched himself from his perch on top of him. The boys began wrestling each other on the floor, while all around them pillows were being swung wildly and bedclothes strewn about the room.

The noise created was tremendous and soon there were other eager faces at the doorway. Many joined in the fun, lashing out freely, until the first adults arrived on the scene.

Lights came on and dozens of eyes blinked at the mess. It looked as though a tornado had whirled through the dormitory, with bodies, pillows, blankets and sleeping bags scattered everywhere like litter.

Slowly the fighters disentangled themselves, tugged their pyjamas back straight and pretended to be

47

busy searching around for lost buttons. The hostel staff were not amused.

'You've got ten minutes to put this room back to rights,' the manager ordered. 'And then we don't want a peep out of anybody for the rest of the night.'

'Andrew, really,' said Grandad. 'I don't need three guesses to know who was behind this little caper.'

Andrew gave him a sheepish grin, but this disappeared instantly when Simon held out his helmet. One of the plastic horns was crumpled, and the back caved in where somebody had trodden on it.

'Hey, look what some clumsy oaf has done to my helmet,' he wailed, but nobody was prepared to give him any sympathy. 'Spent all last week's pocket money on that, I did.'

'Tough,' Dean hissed. 'You're gonna get more than your helmet bashed in tomorrow for this.'

Andrew glared at him, but his attention was drawn to Chris sitting slumped in the corner of the room, holding his fingers to his mouth.

'What's up, our kid?' he asked, going over to see.

There were tears starting to roll down Chris's face. 'I've had my fingers bent back,' he whimpered. 'They hurt something rotten.'

'Oh, brilliant!' said Andrew. 'You must be the first person in the whole country this year to get injured in a pillow fight.'

Only five Vikings eventually trailed moodily back to their own dormitory. Grandad and one of the hostel staff were giving Chris some first aid downstairs.

'Right,' said the manager, making sure they'd all clambered back into their cold beds. 'No more nonsense tonight, you people, or you'll be in big trouble.'

'We already are,' Andrew muttered. 'Looks like we've just gone and lost our goalie.'

'Serves you right,' the man replied, switching off the light and firmly shutting the door behind him.

'And a Happy New Year to you, too, mister,' whispered Simon cheekily as his footsteps disappeared down the corridor.

They all sniggered until Duggie

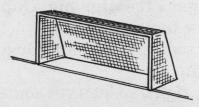

added a warning from the bunk above. 'Let's hope he didn't hear that, Simon, or we might lose you as well. He'd probably have you sent home.'

A smothered giggle escaped across the room.

'What's so funny, Rakesh?' Andrew snapped and then he and the others caught sight of something on his bed glittering in the moonlight.

'You little devil,' chuckled Tim, leaning over the rail. 'How did you manage to get hold of that?'

'Easy, I swiped it when we were all tidying up,' Rakesh explained. 'Wonder when they'll realize they've lost their bowling trophy?'

Andrew allowed himself a smile. 'Well done, Racky, nice work. But I'm not bothered about that thing any longer. It's the big Cup we're after now tomorrow.'

'Later today, you mean,' Duggie corrected him.

'Yeah, right, so let's get some sleep, men,' Andrew yawned. 'We want to get the New Year off to a good start.'

Unfortunately for the captain, the first day of the year was not, in fact, to start out quite the way he might have wished . . .

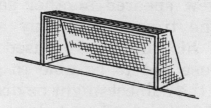

5 *Bathtime*

'How on earth did you get that black eye?'

Andrew shrugged. 'Dunno, Grandad. Must have been in the pillow fight somehow.'

They were eating their Sunday lunch at the hostel and Grandad peered across the table at him suspiciously. 'I didn't notice it at breakfast. Has something happened since that I should know about?'

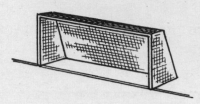

Andrew speared another sausage from the tray and quickly stuffed it into his mouth. He used it as an excuse not to be able to speak, hoping the subject might be dropped. He didn't think Grandad would be best pleased to learn of the incident earlier in United's dressing room . . .

As everyone else filed out to continue the guided tour of the soccer stadium, Andrew and Chris hung back, fascinated by the enormous tiled, sunken bath all the players used after a match.

'Just look at that, our kid, it's almost big enough to swim in. Imagine, one day I could be in there . . .' Andrew breathed dreamily, and then added quickly, 'and you of course as well.'

'You could both be in there sooner than you think.'

The voice came from behind them and carried more of a threat than a promise. The brothers turned slowly round, sensing they had a problem. Six of them in fact. The Demons.

'Well, well, well,' said Andrew. 'And what do you lot want?'

Dean leered. 'We want to pay you back, don't we, lads, for last night. And for pinching our bowling trophy.'

'We gave it back to you this morning,' Chris said.

'So you did, and now we're gonna give you something in return,' Dean cackled. 'A bath! Go get 'em, Demons.'

'No, wait a minute,' Andrew cried quickly. 'Leave my kid brother out of this. It was all my idea and now he's got a bad hand.'

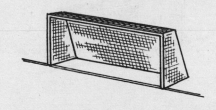

Dean glanced at Chris's bandaged fingers. 'Just hold him, you two,' he said to those on his left. 'He can enjoy watching his big brother having a bath instead.'

Before Chris could make a move, he found himself pinned to the wall by lads either side of him. Andrew made a lunge towards them, but was tackled by the three other Demons while Dean jumped down into the empty bath to insert the plug and turn the taps on full.

Despite Chris's wriggling, he couldn't break free from their grip, and even Andrew found the weight of numbers on top of him too much to cope with. Grabbed around the neck and by the arms, he was being dragged towards the edge of the bath,

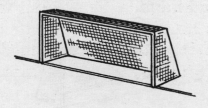

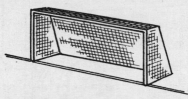

his attackers having to steer clear of his flailing feet.

The Demons hadn't expected such fierce resistance, however, and began to lose their nerve. Not only was the cascading water making a lot of noise, but Chris's yells were also echoing around the room.

'C'mon, hurry up,' Dean cried, turning off the taps with the water still barely ankle deep. 'Let's get out of here before someone comes. Dunk him in quick.'

The Viking captain was struggling so much, they could only slide him over the side before letting go. One of them was too slow. As Andrew toppled, he twisted around to splash down on to his feet, crouched, and yanked the boy in after him, face first.

Chris's guards released him so that they could haul their pal out, but even the Demons had started laughing at his discomfort, with the front of his clothing soaked.

Andrew joined in and couldn't resist making a pun at his rivals' expense. 'Well at least one of you should play a bit *cleaner* now after that early bath.'

'Don't count on it,' Dean sneered. 'You'll get more than just cold feet if we meet again later.'

'Are you all right?' Chris asked, shakily, as the Demons fled.

'Yeah, guess so,' Andrew grunted as he climbed out and squelched away from the bath. 'Eye feels sore, though.'

'You've got a lump over it already.'

'Huh! I've had worse. Load of wimps, those Demons, really. Even old Dean didn't dare tangle with me himself.'

'There's some blood on the tiles, look,' Chris said, pointing out a few red spots near the bath.

'Not mine, wrong colour,' Andrew grinned. 'Viking chiefs have blue blood, like the royals. Must be from that kid I banged heads with.'

He took a final glance round the dressing room. 'I'll be back in here some day, you bet on it. And I just hope that Dean's here too.'

'Why?'

'Cos I'll drown him in that bath, that's why!' Andrew promised. 'C'mon, let's go, we've got a date with him and his mob this afternoon first, if I can do anything about it. They're going to regret this.'

Well though they played, the New Stars never really stood a chance.

It wasn't just the boys' pride at stake, not wanting to be beaten by a group of girls in front of any of United's scouts. After the brothers

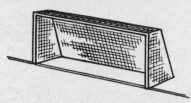

told the rest about the bathroom brawl, the Vikings were all doubly determined to reach the Final.

By the time their game started, they knew the Demons were already waiting for them there. Another school team, Park Primary, had been brushed aside in the first semi-final 3-0, unable to cope with the muscle power of Dean's hit-squad.

Andrew gave a near-perfect performance, breaking up the girls' moves with firm, fair tackles and cutting out any loose passes. The captain was so commanding, Simon was left almost idle until he allowed a long skidding shot to slip through his hands near the end for a consolation goal. He hardly dare look at Andrew, despite the fact that the Vikings were still 3-1 ahead, Duggie's two goals and

Tim's early opener having clinched the match.

The girls' captain shook hands with Andrew and wished him good luck in the Final. She also admired his black eye. 'You've got a beauty there. Who did that?'

Andrew grinned back, a bit embarrassed. 'Oh, just slipped in the bathroom this morning,' he said simply.

She laughed, having heard the rumours about what had taken place at the ground. 'Well, just make sure there's no slip-ups in the Final, right? Nobody wants those bully-boys to win the tournament.'

'Don't worry,' Andrew replied. 'They're tough opponents OK, but we had plenty of Corn Circles for breakfast! We'll be out to run rings round them, showing how football should really be played . . .'

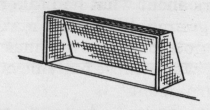

6 Happy New Year?

'Cool it, Duggie, just cool it,' Tim advised.

It hadn't taken long for the Final to see its first foul. As Duggie ran ahead to receive Rakesh's return pass from the kick-off, he was deliberately tripped and sent sprawling.

He sprang up, seeking revenge, but Tim was by his side instantly, grabbing his arm. 'Forget it. If you lose your temper, you can't play properly. That's what they want.'

Duggie snarled, shrugging away from Tim's grasp. 'OK, OK, I'm not gonna hit him – yet.'

Andrew came running up to take the free-kick. 'Tim's right, Duggie. Keep your mind on the game. The best way to hurt this bunch of foulers is to beat them at football, not in a fight.'

It was difficult for Andrew himself to stay calm, but he remembered Grandad's warning before the match. 'Play by the rules. Don't let them drag you down to their level.'

'We won't start anything, Grandad,' he'd promised. But that didn't mean to say he'd allow the Demons to have the last word as well.

Both teams were extra keen in the Final to try and impress United's talent-spotters, but the Vikings failed to find any early rhythm. Just as in their group match, they were soon forced back on the defensive and twice Simon reacted quickly to block goal-bound shots. The Demons were using the occasion well to show off their soccer skills, displaying good ball control

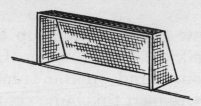

and passing ability. Sadly, however, when they did lose possession, they still tended to spoil things by fouling and complaining loudly every time the referee gave a decision against them.

Grandad was praying the Vikings might be able to hold out till half-time, but as he looked up at the clock, the Demons seized on a mistake and scored.

Rakesh slipped trying to reach a pass and was left helpless as one of their players strode by him with the ball. He switched it quickly to the lurking Dean, whose first effort at goal was charged down by Andrew. His second, from the rebound, scorched past Simon's right hand, hit the top of the inside of the far post and glanced into the net.

Dean immediately went whooping away down the pitch, jumping up into the embrace of his teammates. 'We've won now,' he boasted. 'They won't recover from that. They haven't got the bottle.'

'Keep your heads up,' Grandad said as the Vikings grouped around him at the interval. 'I always reckon the best form of defence is attack. You've got to try and give their keeper some work to do. So far, he's been able to catch up on last night's lost sleep.'

Grandad also pointed out Mr Jones among the spectators. 'He's only just arrived because of the snow on the roads. Let's give him a goal to cheer at least or he might even make us all walk back home!'

They laughed and began the second half in better spirits, catching the Demons by surprise with some lively attacking moves. Duggie found enough space to trouble the goalie at last, and then Tim curled a shot from long range that skimmed over the low crossbar.

Stung into action, the Demons hit back fiercely. Simon had to dive full length to make a good save, and when Dean suddenly broke clear and raced headlong for goal, their victory looked certain. Perhaps the striker thought so too. He hesitated a second before shooting, trying to make sure of scoring, but the delay proved fatal. As he drew his foot back for the killer blow, Andrew pounced.

The Vikings' skipper had chased back desperately and now timed his tackle to perfection. His right foot took the ball away cleanly but the force of their bodies colliding sent Dean crashing heavily to the floor.

'Play on,' ordered the referee, but as Rakesh sprinted away with the loose ball, he was splattered against the boards by a ruthless defender who made no attempt at all to challenge fairly.

The referee stopped the game straightaway to warn the boy, allowing Rakesh to receive attention for a gash on his leg.

'I don't think he ought to carry on with an injury like this,' the first aid man said. 'Have you got a sub?'

Grandad blew out his cheeks. 'Well, sort of,' he said. 'We've got a spare goalie.'

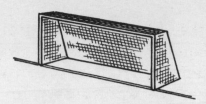

'Chris'll have to come on, Grandad,' Andrew put in. 'At least he can run, which is more than Rakesh can do for a bit. We can't be a man short against this crew.'

Chris began to protest half-heartedly. 'I'm no good on the field, Grandad. I'm a goalie.'

'Not now, you're not,' Grandad said. 'C'mon, get that tracksuit off – you're on. Play up front with Duggie and keep on the move. Give their defenders somebody else to worry about.'

His marker, however, did not seem very concerned. 'We meet again, squirt,' he taunted. 'Want a busted leg to go with your hand?'

Chris tried to ignore him. He felt very strange playing out on the pitch and every time the ball came his

way, others easily beat him to it.
The seconds were ticking away, but
it all depended on how many extra
ones the referee would add on for
Rakesh's injury and also to make
up for the time-wasting tactics the
Demons were now using.

They seemed more interested in
kicking the ball out of play or passing
back to their goalie than in trying
to increase their lead. Pressure on
the Vikings was relaxed and Andrew
urged his men forward in search of an
equalizer.

'C'mon, we can't let them win,' he
called. 'They don't deserve it.'

Good fortune, happily, was on their
side. As the referee studied his watch,
Tim received the ball wide on the left.
Dummying to go down the boards, he
jinked inside on to his right foot and
let fly at goal.

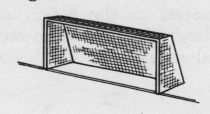

His hurried shot sliced across the front of the area, but a groan died in his throat when the ball struck Chris's knee and took a massive deflection past the stranded goalkeeper. The Demons' goalie threw himself backwards in despair but failed to stop the ball crossing the line.

Chris had barely realized what had happened before his elder brother lifted him off his feet. 'Super sub!' Andrew screamed into his ear. 'You've done it for us. We're level!'

During the break before a short period of extra time began, Chris lapped up the fuss, showing the exact spot where the ball had made contact. 'I shall never wash that knee again,' he laughed.

Duggie, however, was too busy gloating to examine the famous knee, staring across at where the Demons lay slumped on the floor. 'Look at them, they're finished. They reckoned it was all over.'

'Well, it will be soon,' Andrew declared. 'We've got 'em now. C'mon, the Vikings!'

His battle cry sent them back on full of confidence and for the first time in both their encounters, the Vikings were on top. Now it was the Demons who were struggling to survive and Simon became almost a spectator, rarely having a touch of the ball.

Duggie rattled the boards behind the goal with one shot, Tim unluckily shaved a post with another, and such one-way attacking traffic seemed certain to bring its reward.

It was Andrew who began the crucial move, and the captain himself had the thrill of finishing it, too, in great style. Taking the ball off a sulky Dean in his own half, he laid it out

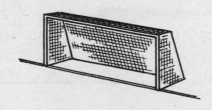

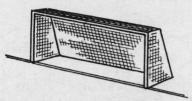

wide to Duggie and continued his run forward for the cross. When it came, he met it smack on the volley with his right foot, lashing the ball past the goalkeeper to bulge out the back of the netting with its power.

'The winner!' he screamed, daring anyone to challenge his verdict.

Nobody did. The Demons had lost heart completely and at the final whistle soon afterwards, Andrew leapt high into the air and then suddenly raced off the pitch.

'Where's he off to?' Grandad wondered aloud.

'I think I know,' grinned Rakesh. 'He'll be back any minute.'

When Andrew did reappear, he was wearing his Viking helmet, rescued from his sports bag for just this moment. The magic moment at the

presentation ceremony when he was able to lift the silver trophy above its battered, curved horns and his glistening black eye.

'Well, I'll say one thing,' Mr Jones remarked to Grandad as they applauded. 'Your Andrew certainly looks the part in that helmet. He's obviously been in the wars a bit this weekend.'

'Aye, he's a real battler, all right,' the old man chuckled proudly. 'And that shiner isn't the only souvenir he'll take home either. I've heard he's also been named Player of the Tournament!'

After the Vikings had received their individual medals, Andrew was able to show everyone his prized certificate. 'That was the biggest, most important goal I've ever scored,' he told the headmaster. 'It meant so much to beat those Demons and earn this.'

'Andrew and Tim have been picked out by the scouts, too,' Chris piped up excitedly. 'United are running a special coaching course at Easter for all those they've liked the look of here.'

Mr Jones nodded with pleasure at Andrew. 'What a tremendous opportunity, young man! Now that's what I really call a big goal for you to aim at – making your dream of becoming a professional footballer start to come true.'

Andrew turned and grinned at his younger brother. 'Dean got invited too, you know. I wonder how well he can swim?'

Chris burst out laughing, but neither Grandad nor Mr Jones had any idea what the boys' little private joke was all about!

THE END

APPENDIX

Five-a-Side Tournament – Results and Scorers

Group A

Dean's Demons	5 – 1	City Boys
(Duggie, Rakesh) Vikings	2 – 1	Lynfield Rd Juniors
Dean's Demons	2 – 0	Vikings
City Boys	2 – 2	Lynfield Rd Juniors
Lynfield Rd Juniors	1 – 3	Dean's Demons
(Tim 3, Duggie) Vikings	4 – 0	City Boys

Group A Table

	Played	Won	Drawn	Lost	Goals For	Against	Points
Demons	3	3	0	0	10	2	6
Vikings	3	2	0	1	6	3	4
Juniors	3	0	1	2	4	7	1
City Boys	3	0	1	2	3	11	1

Group B

New Stars	3 – 0	Famous Five
Park Primary	3 – 3	Saints
New Stars	2 – 2	Park Primary
Famous Five	1 – 1	Saints
Saints	2 – 2	New Stars
Park Primary	2 – 0	Famous Five

Group B Table

	Played	Won	Drawn	Lost	Goals For	Against	Points
New Stars	3	1	2	0	7	4	4
Park Primary	3	1	2	0	7	5	4
Saints	3	0	3	0	6	6	3
Famous Five	3	0	1	2	1	6	1

Semi-Finals

Dean's Demons   3 – 0   Park Primary
(Duggie 2, Tim)   Vikings   3 – 1   New Stars

FINAL

(Chris, Andrew)   Vikings   2 – 1   Dean's Demons
(after extra-time)

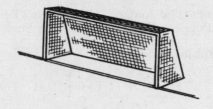